ROCK HAPPY 2

Dissonant

Chris Spence

For my Mum.

1 | Chaos

"My name is John—"

"I don't care what your name is. I want to know what's going on. Why does this place look so bad? Why won't my MeChip work?"

The man who had interrupted John Locke was standing at the front of the crowd. His eyes had a wild, almost furtive look, but his voice sounded angry. *He's scared*, Alex thought as he looked down from the stage. *He's scared but trying to hide it.*

"Please let me speak. I can explain everything," Locke replied, holding up his hands for silence and raising his voice as he talked into the microphone.

"I am Dr. John Locke. I once worked for Happy Corps. I invented the MeChip each of you has inserted in the back of your necks."

"If you're such an expert, why isn't mine working?" the angry man yelled. "Who else's MeChip is broken?" he asked, turning to face the crowd.

A thousand hands rose into the air as people began talking anxiously to their neighbors. Alex could see the man's fear and confusion reflected in every single face in the auditorium. Again, Locke tried to calm them.

"Your MeChips have been disabled," Locke said, speaking still more loudly into the microphone and seeking to silence the crowd. "They have been disabled because the technology they contain was being used to control you."

"What are you talking about?" the man shouted.

"The MeChips were once a technological force for good—like your old smartphone, flatscreen tv and virtual reality console from days past all rolled into one. But for many years now the government has been using them to feed false memories and images into your brain, to show you a world that isn't real. President Davison and the other elites want you to believe you're living in a golden age, that life is good for all Americans," he declared, looking earnestly at the sea of faces.

"What the MeChip has been showing you is false. There is no promised land. Our waters are contaminated and our air is polluted. Our country lies in ruins, diseased and devastated. While the elites live in luxury, your lives are being destroyed. Democracy is dead. Your health and freedom have been ripped from you by the MeChip and the phony, rose-tinted images it feeds you every minute of every day."

"That's why this school auditorium looks so run down and old. This school, this city, is dirty and decaying. The MeChip was hiding all of that from you. Fortunately, Alex and his band were able to break the MeChips' control with their music. One of its few flaws is it cannot cope with beautiful music played on real instruments. Alex and his friends helped short circuit your MeChips and free you of its control," Dr. Locke stated, turning to nod approvingly at his young companion.

"You're nuts! This is crazy talk," the man shouted. Others in the crowd nodded or murmured their agreement.

"I wish you were right," Locke replied. "But if you don't believe me, at least believe your own eyes. Look around at what you see now the MeChip is not in control. Look at this hall. Look at your neighbors."

Alex watched them closely as the crowd stared up at the cracked window panes and peeling paint, as they cast uncertain glances at the people around them; at their neighbors, friends, and family. Instead of the fashionable clothes projected by the MeChip, people were now shabbily dressed, their garments tattered and old. In many cases, their healthy glow had gone, replaced by tired, wan complexions and gaunt faces. Some citizens looked seriously sick.

Many in the audience appeared on the edge of panic. They were wide-eyed and alarmed, obviously unable to fully comprehend Locke's message.

"Please listen to me!" Locke said, raising his voice again. "This may be hard to accept, but I can help you understand. I have a plan to fix all of this. What we need to do now is—"

Fzzoom! Fzzoom! Fzzoom!

Without warning a dozen laser beams blasted through the open doors at the back of the hall. They struck into the rear of the crowd, smashing into people—into Alex's friends and neighbors—sending them sprawling to the ground.

For a millisec, there was a stunned silence. Then panic gripped the crowd as a dozen or more troops burst through the entrance. Several hurled smoke canisters into the crowd, which backed away, pushing and shoving in a desperate effort to evade their attackers.

From the stage, Alex, Locke, Abby, and the others stared in disbelief.

"How did they get here so soon?" Locke muttered to himself.

"Attention citizens!" came an amplified voice from the back of the hall. "This is the Regulators. You are part of an unlawful assembly. Surrender yourselves now for questioning and no one else need be hurt."

Alex saw every possible reaction from the crowd. Some put their hands above their heads, instantly obeying. Several young children burst into tears, covering their eyes or burying their heads into their mom's or dad's bodies, seeking comfort. Others tried to escape, running towards side doors or clambering through windows.

Alex's elderly English teacher, Ms. Monroe, was the bravest. She began hitting one of the Regs with her handbag. Moments later, she was joined by at least a dozen more—men and women, boys and girls—who began fighting, punching and kicking, pushing and shoving at the invaders, trying to force them back.

But they were unarmed and outmatched. Alex saw Regs—the regular cops—and several Fixers begin blasting away at the crowd indiscriminately, knocking more people down. Alex prayed their weapons were set to stun, not kill.

"We should leave, now. Right, John?" Alex shouted over the tumult.

Alex's question shook the old man out of his momentary paralysis.

"Yes ... of course. You're right, Alex. If we fight back, we risk hitting more innocent people," he yelled, shaking his grizzled head. "And there are too many. Is there a way out behind the stage?"

"Follow me." Alex instantly turned to the others on the platform. There were more than a dozen people there: his parents, Abby, Iggy and his mom, Sol and Tom, plus members of several of the other bands that had been competing and had emerged from backstage.

"We need to escape!" he bellowed above the din. "Come on."

Some nodded, while others looked unsure.

"No way, man. I've gotta find my mom," yelled Eric Block, the drummer in Iggy's band. He jumped off the stage and into the crowd as a laser blast passed just inches above his head. A couple of other band members followed him, leaping like lemmings into the panicked mass. Meanwhile, some folks in the crowd were clambering *onto* the stage to escape the advancing Regs and Fixers. It was chaos.

There was no time to waste, Alex decided, as more laser beams sprayed around the hall. This was not the moment for talking, for persuading people to come with him. Whoever wanted to would follow.

He led the way quickly towards the back of the stage, stooping almost without thinking to grab the X-guitar he'd performed with just minutes earlier and strapping it across his back as he ran. Once backstage, Alex led them down the nearest corridor, just ahead of Locke, Abby, his parents, and at least a dozen others.

"Here, take this," Locke said as he drew alongside his young protégé. Alex felt something bulky pressed into his hand and saw, with astonishment, a laser gun. "I took it from one of General Arnold's Fixers. Don't worry, it's set to stun." Alex saw Locke hand two more weapons to his mother and father, who were just behind.

Alex led them around one corner, then another, barely noticing how different the corridors looked without the MeChip's rose-tinted view, not registering the rusty lockers or peeling paint. Rapidly, he retraced his steps from earlier in the evening when he'd snuck into the school. Behind them he could hear shrieks and screams, the ceaseless sound of lasers, then a louder blast that shook dust off the beams in the ceiling. But there was no sign of pursuit. Finally, they reached an exterior door that led to the bike sheds. Alex stopped.

"We're at the back of the main building. Where now?" Alex asked, turning to Locke.

"We've got to reach the forest," Locke panted as he tried to catch his breath. "Can you get us there?"

"Yes," Alex nodded. "Across the football field and over the train tracks."

"Then let's go."

Alex cautiously pushed open the door and stepped outside, his right hand gripping the gun.

Nothing. All seemed quiet. The group made its way around the edge of the rear school yard, then advanced slowly onto the darkened pitch.

2 | The Chase

Two beams of blinding light illuminated the field, enveloping them in a circle of white. Alex raised one hand, squinting as he tried to see what—or who—had them in their sights.

"This is the Regs! Place your hands above your heads and kneel on the ground," came an amplified voice from somewhere up ahead.

The group hesitated, looking to Alex and Locke for answers.

Before they could even speak a laser blast struck into their midst. Alex turned and saw his mother reel as the shot shattered the gun Locke had given her, smashing it out of her grip and sending it spinning behind them as she gasped in pain and surprise and stared, open-mouthed, at her hand. Alex saw a deep cut on her palm and a stream of blood already blossoming out of it and spilling onto the grass.

"I said hands up. Now!" The voice came from the direction of the piercing beams of light.

Incensed, without even pausing to think, Alex raised his gun and fired. His shot flew to the right, well wide of the mark. Instantly he fired again, this time hitting one of the two targets. Alex heard a smashing sound, like broken glass, from about fifty paces away.

Locke fired, too. His blast struck the second source of the light, plunging them into darkness.

"Run. Run. Now! Make for the trees," Alex ordered the group.

Roused into action, the others started sprinting towards the distant forest as laser blasts began cutting through the air.

Around him, Alex heard the pounding of feet and the ragged breathing of friends and family as they ran for their lives. Without their lights, the Regs' aim suffered as several blasts flew to the left or right of the fleeing band.

Another shot struck just feet away. Alex heard a cry and saw a figure stumble and fall in the darkness. He tried to slow his pace, intending to turn back and help whoever it was, but felt fingers grip his arm, dragging him onwards.

"Don't stop, Alex. If you stop, you'll be hit," Locke panted, urging him on.

Reluctantly Alex complied, breaking once more into a run, wondering who'd been struck, hoping he wouldn't be the next to go down. As laser beams flashed to the left and right, he thought he heard another cry of pain from a little way behind him. Oh, smeck! Had someone else been hit? He couldn't be sure and all the while Locke was by his side urging him on.

They kept running. Alex risked a quick glance over his shoulder and saw his mother just behind, with Abby a few steps back. Others were on either side of them but it was hard to make out who they were in the darkness. Was that Tom's lanky frame silhouetted against the dark sky?

They had made it across the fields and reached the train tracks. Alex rushed across, then pulled up for a moment to help Locke, who was breathing heavily.

"Are you okay, John?"

"I'll be fine. But you must lead the others now. Go to the edge of the forest and wait for me there. I'll stay here and join you after I've taken care of whoever's still following us," instructed the old man, his breath coming in gasps.

"But why? We're getting away," Alex said, confused. The sounds of pursuit had receded and it was clear there were only one or two Regs now chasing them. The flash of lasers had become more intermittent, less accurate, as the darkness continued to hinder their pursuers.

"We need to make sure they don't follow us into the forest. Trust me, Alex. You must lead the others," Locke said, sensing Alex's hesitation.

"Alright. Come on everyone, up to the trees," Alex whispered as loud as he dared to the small knot of people now crossing the tracks.

Without waiting for a reply, he turned and made his way across the old road and up into the fields. He could hear the others close behind, hear their labored breathing and stumbling footsteps as they struggled up the steep hill trying to navigate bushes and the uneven ground in the pale moonlight. After another minute or two they reached the nearest trees, thin and spread out on the forest's edge. Alex stopped and turned.

"What now?" asked a voice he thought might be Sol's.

"We wait," Alex instructed, speaking as loud as he dared.

Before anyone could speak again, there was a flash of light from below as a laser fired a single shot, followed a millisec later by another close by. The first flew straight and low, momentarily illuminating the train tracks near the spot where they'd left Locke. The second beam burst directly upwards, shooting into the sky before fizzling out a hundred yards above them, like a cheap firework.

What had happened? Was Locke alright?

Before Alex could even think about it, however, he felt a hand on his arm.

"It's me, Mom."

Alex breathed a sigh of relief. She was alright. She'd made it. He hugged her, noticing as he did so that she was trembling. Or was it he who was shaking? He realized he'd have to pull himself together if he was going to be any use at all. After all, he'd had more time to come to terms with the truth about their MeChips. They would need him to stay calm.

"Who else is here?" Alex asked, trying to keep the fear out of his voice and make faces out in the darkness.

"It's me, Abby," said another voice from close by. Alex let out another breath, felt another rush of gratitude.

Others stepped forward and spoke as Alex began to put faces to names and his eyes adjusted to the darkness. Sol and Tom were both there. So were Iggy and his mom, Alice. Two of Iggy's bandmates, Frank Delius and Eddy Dent, had made it, as had Harriet, the brilliant bass player from *Saratoga Redux*. Abby's friend Sybil was here, too. And so was Abby's mom, Susanna.

But there was no sign of her dad. Nor, Alex realized in shock, was his own father among the group.

"I've got to find my dad," Abby said the instant she realized he wasn't there.

"Me too. I don't know where either of my parents are," said Sybil, her voice high-pitched and tremulous. Others nodded their agreement. Frank Delius and Eddy Dent moved as if to head back down the hill to the school, but Alex stepped in front of them.

"No way. It's too dangerous down there."

As if to prove his point, the sound of screams carried on the wind from down in the valley, while a burst of laser blasts lit up the school. Then another sound intruded, getting louder by the second.

Whup-whup-whup-whup-whup.

Everyone was silent, straining to make out what it was.

"A helicopter," Sol whispered.

He was right. Alex recognized the sound of rotor blades in the distance. A powerful searchlight blinked on out of nowhere and they finally all saw the chopper above the school as its bright beam began sweeping across the parking lot, illuminating everything it touched.

For a moment, no one moved. Then someone brushed past Alex and started running back down the hill.

"I have to find them! I have to find my parents," came a voice as a shadowy figure was swallowed by darkness.

"That was Eddy. We should join him," Iggy said urgently. "We all need to go help, go find people's parents."

"No. Dr. Locke said we should wait for him here," Alex insisted. "I mean, look at it down there. What good could we do against all those Regs?"

"We can do more good down there than up here," Iggy persisted. "And where's the old man now? You saw that laser blast. He probably got shot like the others. We have to decide for ourselves now. And I say we go back!"

Iggy's voice had become almost a growl. Several of the others muttered their agreement. Alex ignored them.

"And do what?" he replied. "Look, I want to find my dad, too. But we'll get massacred down there."

"We can fight, can't we?" Iggy said. "Who's with me?"

"Locke said to stay here and that's what I'm going to do," Alex insisted.

"Alright, stay then. I don't care. But I'm going back. Give me your gun," Iggy said, taking a step towards his old adversary.

"What?"

"You won't need it if you're skulking around up here. But I will. Give it to me." He took another step forward. He was so close now Alex could see his head and shoulders silhouetted clearly against the sky, although his face remained in shadow. Alex could feel himself tense up. What should he do?

Before he could reply there was a cracking sound from somewhere below as a twig snapped. Everyone froze.

"Alex? Abby? Are you there? I need your help."

It was Locke. With a rush of relief, Alex hurried forward, his eyes straining to see his friend. Abby and Iggy joined him and they made their way cautiously back down the uneven pasture, finally making out Locke in the dim light.

But something didn't seem right. As Alex came closer, Locke's shadowy figure looked misshapen and oddly large. He seemed to be struggling to stand up.

Alex dashed forward and realized what it was.

"Dad!" he said, understanding now he was closer that it was not one man, but two, walking side-by-side.

His relief turned to shock, though, as Alex saw his father leaning heavily against the older man.

"What happened? Are you alright, Dad?"

"I think a laser caught him a glancing blow," Locke answered. "I found him on the ground a few yards behind the tracks. He should be alright but he needs our help."

Together, Alex and Iggy propped up Alex's dad, who seemed only half-conscious. Meanwhile, Abby had her arm around Locke, who was breathing heavily.

"Are you okay, Dr. Locke?" she asked.

"Just a little tired from today's events. I'll survive."

"Come on. Let's go," Alex said.

The small group made its way slowly up the hill. Finally, they reached the others.

"Alex, is that you?" his mother's voice came from out of the darkness.

"Yes, and we've got Dad," Alex replied.

"Ben? Oh, Ben! Are you alright?" She ran forward and seized him in a tight embrace.

"I'm fine," he gasped, although he didn't sound it. "Just need to sit down ... catch my breath," he muttered as Alex's mom started fussing over him.

He wasn't the only one in bad shape. Locke had also sunk down and was sitting on a small boulder, badly winded. Alex heard a sob and saw Sybil with her head in her hands. Tom was patting her on the back trying to console her.

"What's happening down there?" asked Iggy's mom Alice.

"It's ... not good," Locke replied after a short pause. "I managed to stop the Reg who was still on our trail, but I think they're rounding up everyone at the school."

"Then we should go help," Iggy repeated. "Some of us have family back there. We need to get them out of danger."

"You can't," Locke said, his voice stronger now.

"Why not?" Iggy demanded aggressively.

"Because there are dozens of Regs at the school. More will be arriving. They've even got a helicopter. If you go back, you'll just end up sharing the fate of those we left behind."

"But we have to do something!" Iggy said fiercely.

"We will do something. We will escape and live to fight another day."

"So we just leave our friends and family to be captured, maybe even killed?"

"Yes and no."

"What's that supposed to mean?"

"Yes, we have to leave them for now. To go back without any hope, without any sort of plan, would be suicidal. But we must also pray we are *not* leaving them to perish."

"What?"

"I think ... I hope ... the Regs have set their weapons to stun, not to kill."

"How do you know?"

"I don't. Not for sure. But logic tells me they wouldn't wish to kill these people, not when they can be reprogrammed."

"And that's the best you've got, old man?"

"Yes, Iggy Elgar, it is," Locke said, his voice firm. "We escape now and live to fight another day. And we pray the people down there can remain safe until we are strong enough—and prepared enough—to actually help them."

"I still think we should go and fight," Iggy said.

"And I can't stop you, young man. Go if you wish. But if you really want to help them, you'll come with me."

"Go where? What's your plan?"

"I am glad you asked. I have a cabin in the woods not too far from here. It is well hidden and has food and other supplies. It will be a squeeze for a group this size but it will offer us shelter and somewhere to hide from our pursuers while we decide our next steps. Who will come with me?"

"I will," Alex said instantly.

"Me too," Abby's mom declared a millisec later.

"And me," came several other voices.

"I will, too," said Iggy's mom.

Only Iggy remained silent as the others looked from him to Locke and back again.

"Alright, fine!" he agreed at last. "But only because my mom's going. And I want one of the guns," he added aggressively.

"Here, take this," Alex's dad sighed, passing the weapon to Iggy in the dark. "I'm in no shape to be using it."

"Good. Then let's do this before I change my mind," Iggy said, holding the weapon tightly.

"Very well," said Locke, apparently satisfied. "Follow me, please," he instructed as he rose slowly to his feet and began to lead them through the forest.

3 | The Cabin

Locke led them a little deeper into the woods. The trees grew closer here but there was still enough moonlight to guide them. Turning to the right, he began skirting the edge of the forest as it circled the town.

Soon the sound of lasers and distant cries dwindled, although once they heard the *whup-whup-whup* of the helicopter as it flew close to where they were, its searchlight strafing the outer trees as it rushed past before banking off in the direction of the town.

Alex felt immense relief that Locke had brought them a little deeper among the trees. If he hadn't—if they had stayed at the very edge—the helicopter would have spotted them and they would already have been discovered. As it was, the group was left shaken but safe.

Not that "shaken" really did it justice, Alex realized as he looked around him. They were disoriented, even panicked. Sybil had to stop more than once as bouts of uncontrollable tears overcame her. Tom, who had been trying to console her, was clearly out of his depth, but Iggy and Abby's moms came to the rescue, calming her after a few minutes so they could at least continue their journey.

Alex and his mom busied themselves helping Alex's dad, who was still unsteady on his feet. Sol, Tom, and Harriet walked in silence, seemingly too shocked by the evening's events to speak. Iggy and his bandmate, Frank Delius, were lagging behind, muttering and whispering conspiratorially. Meanwhile, Abby was up ahead with Locke. She had an arm around the old man's shoulder. His breathing was labored and he was walking slowly.

Alex couldn't be sure how long this journey in the dark lasted. Was it an hour? Two? More? Finally, Locke called a halt.

Alex looked around, catching his breath. The place seemed much like everywhere else, with trees all around them, their shadows ominous and sinister in the night. Beyond the forest, he could just make out the twin smokestacks of the Bright Green Mining company, closer than before and still spewing black clouds of smoke into the air, even at this late hour. A pall of smog still lay over the town below, just visible in the darkness. Nearby was a field with a single tree, its branches leafless and bare.

Something about this spot evidently meant something to Locke, however. "This way," he instructed, leading them further into the forest. "And watch your step. It will be darker in here."

The group advanced carefully as their visibility reduced under the thickening canopy. Alex could hear those around him quite clearly now: the snapping of twigs and crunching of leaves underfoot; Locke's wheezing gasp ahead; Sybil's sniffles and sighs just behind; and Iggy's secretive whispers to Frank Delius bringing up the rear. They walked a little way—perhaps 200 steps at most—before emerging unexpectedly into a clearing. In the moonlight, Alex could see a few large boulders sprinkled haphazardly here and there, and a steep rise up ahead. There was no sign of a cabin, though.

"Wait here all of you. I will be back soon," the old man instructed as he walked slowly away. A moment later he entered the trees on the far side of the glade and was swallowed up by the darkness.

No one spoke. Alex's parents sat down on one of the rocks. Sol and Harriet stood perfectly still, their faces in shadow. Tom began rubbing his hands together to keep warm. Sybil seemed in shock. She was swaying slightly from side to side. Iggy's mom still had an arm around her. After a couple of minutes, Abby turned around and stepped closer to Alex.

"You okay?" she asked in an undertone.

"I'm not sure," Alex replied quietly. "So much has happened; it's hard to take it all in. You?"

"Not really. What that man did to us—General Arnold—it was horrible. Like a nightmare."

"I'm sorry. Really sorry," Alex said, not sure how to reply. He wanted to reach out and put his arm around her, try to comfort her, but before he could work up the courage someone interrupted.

It was Iggy. He had emerged from the darkness and was standing in front of Alex and Abby, hands on hips, gun in his belt. Frank Delius was by his side.

"You okay, Abby?" he asked, placing a hand on her shoulder.

"I guess," she said slowly. Nodding as if satisfied, he turned towards Alex.

"Where's the old man got to now, Franklin?"

"He's gone to find the cabin, I guess," Alex answered, surprised.

"Then why not take all of us? Why leave us here?"

"I ... don't know," Alex confessed.

"You don't know? You're asking us to trust this guy and you don't know what he's doing or where he is?"

"Yes. I'm not sure where he's gone but I do trust him," Alex said. He was finding it hard to think. He was so tired, so overwhelmed by everything that had happened, and now Locke was gone and Iggy had just put his hand on Abby's shoulder and was asking questions he, Alex, couldn't answer. "He'll be back," Alex said, trying to sound reassuring rather than irritated.

"What if he doesn't come back?" Sybil said suddenly, her voice high and agitated. "What if we just end up stuck in this forest forever? I wish my mom and dad were here! I wish things were back to normal ... back to how it was before."

She raised her hands to her face and started sobbing. Once again, Iggy and Abby's moms tried to calm her.

"Nice one, Iggy," Sol said, stepping forward. "Way to help calm things down."

"Hey, I'm just saying what we're all thinking," he said, holding up his hands. "We have no idea what this old guy is up to or even where he's gone—"

"The old guy is right here." John Locke emerged from the trees holding an ancient lamp that cast a thin glow around him. "And the cabin is ready for you. Come. I have shelter and warmth and blankets—everything we need."

Locke led the group across the clearing and among the far trees. They walked another thirty paces or so before reaching what appeared to be the bottom of a small cliff. Locke steered them to the left, skirting the edge of the cliff's base. Then he stopped. Pulling back some foliage, the group saw a small door built into the rock. Locke tugged it open and stepped aside for them to enter.

"Watch your heads," he warned as they entered in single file through the low, wooden doorway. Alex led the way down a short corridor flanked by rock walls that ended at a second door. Slivers of light were streaming around the edges and through a keyhole. Wondering what he'd find on the other side, Alex turned the handle and entered.

The light was so bright, so unexpected, that for a few moments he could see nothing at all. Shielding his eyes against the brilliance, he crossed the threshold and stepped aside so the others could follow.

Finally, his vision adjusted and the room began to take shape. It was a biggish space, part cabin, part cave, but cozy enough in its own way. Two bright lamps were burning on a broad mantelpiece above a fireplace, which crackled with burning wood against the far wall. A large kettle was hanging above it, the flames licking the metal. Steam was beginning to stream from its spout. The left wall was covered in shelves stacked with every imaginable item—from tinned food to ropes, blankets to bottles, books to batteries to old walkie-talkies and other electronic gear. There were even a couple of ancient hunting rifles, a bow, and some arrows. By the opposite wall stood a small desk and chair as well as an ancient leather couch. At the far end of the room was another door.

Soon everyone had entered, most crowding together near the entrance. Iggy and Frank approached the fire, warming their hands in the heat. Alex's mom led his dad to the couch. He sat down heavily, leaned back, and closed his eyes. Locke was the last to come in. He had already closed the exterior door. Now he shut this one, barring it with a stout piece of wood.

"Alright, old-timer. We're here. What now?" Iggy asked.

"Now, young man, we rest."

"We rest?"

"Yes."

"And that's your plan?"

"No. But my plan—or should I say our plan, for it is one we must make together—will be improved by some sleep."

Iggy looked like he wanted to say more but Locke held up a hand for silence.

"I would love to hear your ideas, Iggy Elgar, but it is clear we need sleep first. I, for one, am exhausted."

"And where are we supposed to sleep, exactly? I don't think thirteen of us would fit on that couch," Iggy said sarcastically.

"Quite right. The door over there leads to a small room. It has a bed of no great size, but it could accommodate a couple of us at least. I suggest Ben and Liz Franklin take it, since both of them have been injured. Sybil, perhaps you should take the couch, since you look like you need a good night's sleep more than anyone. As for the rest of us, we will have to make do with blankets and this floor. It may not be perfect, but it will be warm enough and certainly better than being outside in the forest. And now, who would like a cup of hot chocolate?"

It was like a scene from a disaster movie: windows smashed, chairs overturned, walls pockmarked and blackened in a hundred different places from laser blasts, the floor wet with blood.

He stepped outside and grimaced as the morning sunlight struck his face. A few yards away the burned-out husk of a car lay on its side, its windows shattered and wisps of smoke still curling out of its engine. A black van pulled up and several Regs got out, saluting him smartly as they trotted into the school auditorium through its battered and broken doors.

Slade Arnold rubbed the back of his head and scowled. Whoever had hit him had left a lump the size of an egg. His head pounded, his mouth felt dry as sandpaper, and his body ached. At some point, he knew, he would need to rest. But not now. Not yet. There was still too much to do.

His plan had failed. At least he had had the presence of mind to call in reinforcements before he had been knocked out. He shuddered to think what would have happened if he hadn't. Still, it was bad enough. Just where were Locke and the Franklins and the Elgars now? And what the smeck would the president say?

As if on cue, his headset began to ring, its tone shrill and insistent. He paused for a moment, swallowing hard as he tried to compose himself, forcing his face into one of its rare smiles. Only then did he pick up.

"Good morning, Madam President. To what do I owe the pleasure?"

4 | Plans and Plots

Alex rubbed his eyes and yawned. He had slept badly, his body unaccustomed to a hard floor and sharing a room with so many others, several of whom snored. He had a crick in his neck and a dull ache in his lower back. Still, he had spent the night in a warm, safe place, which was better than many of the alternatives.

As he looked around the room—at the circle of people sitting or standing in Locke's hideout, their faces flickering in the light cast by the newly-made fire—he wondered if they felt as fatigued or disoriented as he did. His parents actually looked better for the night's repose, although both bore signs of yesterday's drama. His father had a bandage wrapped around his forehead, hiding the wound he'd received from the laser's glancing blow. His mother's palm was similarly strapped from where the gun had been blasted out of her hand. They were sitting on the couch next to Sybil, who also looked a little better from a night's sleep, although her eyes remained red-rimmed. Tom was sitting on the other side of her, casting furtive glances in her direction as if worried she might relapse.

Meanwhile, Iggy was leaning against the mantelpiece close to his mother, Abby, and his friend Frank, who was yawning loudly, mouth wide open. As Alex looked at Iggy, his rival leaned over and whispered something to Abby, who frowned but nodded slowly. What was *that* all about, he wondered? But his thoughts were interrupted as Locke, with help from Harriet, Sol, and Abby's mom, started serving coffee and oatmeal cookies.

"I'm sorry I can't offer a more appetizing breakfast," Locke said apologetically.

"A coffee and a cookie are just what I need right now—thank you," Alex's mom said, while several of the others nodded their agreement.

"Better than nothing," Iggy muttered just loud enough for the others to hear. No one replied, although Frank smirked and Iggy's mom cast her son a disapproving look.

For a moment there was silence as the group gratefully drank their coffee or nibbled on a cookie. Finally, Locke broke the silence.

"Now we have slept and hopefully recovered a little from yesterday's events, it is time for us to decide what to do next. I suggest we—"

"Wait up," interrupted Iggy. "I want an explanation of what's going on first. What the smeck happened last night? I know you started to tell us, but I for one am still confused."

"A fair question, Mr. Elgar," Locke replied. There was a pause as Dr. Locke gathered his thoughts.

"As I said last night, the MeChip is not the force for good it should be. For many years now it has been used to influence and control you, feeding you false images and ideas."

Locke proceeded to repeat the tale he had told Alex earlier: from the decision by President Davison Senior to steal the election fifteen years ago to Locke's realization that music—if played particularly well and on real instruments—could short-circuit the MeChip and break its control.

"So you wanted to free 1000 people in a high-school auditorium? What good would that do?" Iggy asked, interrupting once more.

"Actually, my plan was to broadcast the performance to every MeChip in America using a transmitter I'd created that could circumvent Happy Corps' control. Unfortunately, General Arnold caught me before I could put the plan into operation."

"So you failed?"

"Yes."

"At least we're all free," Tom said, scowling at Iggy.

"Yes we are," Locke said. "And that is all thanks to you, Tom—and to Sol and Alex here—who played so well it short-circuited the MeChips of everyone in the auditorium. I could not have been more impressed," Locke said, smiling.

"Well ... um ... you're welcome, Dr. L.," Tom said, his pale face turning beetroot red. "Although if I'm honest I didn't know that's what I was doing. I thought Alex had gone all Crazy-Clinton again with his old instruments and sheet music. But you know how he is—he seemed so determined I just went along with it."

"Then we should all thank you for trusting your friend," Locke said.

"Why?" Iggy interrupted. "I mean, what's better about this? We're in a cave in the woods when we could have been back in our homes, safe and sound."

"You'd be living a lie!" Alex burst in, unable to believe his ears.

"And you would not, I'm afraid, be safe," Locke added before Iggy could respond. "No one is really safe with such a corrupt and evil government in charge."

"A government you helped take power," Iggy shot back.

"Yes, I cannot deny it. It is a dishonor and a disgrace I have to live with every day."

"Yes, but you're doing something about it now," Alex said defensively, glaring at Iggy.

"The question is, what do we do next?" asked Harriet, brows furrowed.

There was silence for a moment before Iggy spoke again.

"I would have thought that was *uber* obvious. If you're all set on breaking the MeChip's control—which I'm still not sure is a great idea, by the way—then why not go back to the old man's original idea? Let's just find a way to broadcast music to everyone."

Alex opened his mouth to argue, then closed it again. He looked around at the others, saw Locke nodding slowly. Reluctantly, Alex realized Iggy was right. Locke already had a plan to free people of the MeChip's hold. Why not use it?

The question, of course, was how?

"Your status report, captain?"

"Yes, General. We've secured the area and almost all civilians are now accounted for. The survivors are being reprocessed and a clean-up squad is on its way. More Fixers will arrive from regional headquarters within the hour."

"And how many civilians are still missing?"

"Thirteen, General."

"And no leads?"

"Not yet, sir."

"What about the boy you recaptured later in the night? The one spotted near the football field?"

"We don't know yet. He's still unconscious from the injuries he sustained fighting the Regs. We had the helicopter conduct a sweep of the area, but they saw nothing."

"Then what about the civilians' MeChips? Surely they can't all have burned out?" General Arnold demanded, a note of exasperation entering his voice.

"I'm sorry, General. They short-circuited. Every single one."

"But there has to be a way to trace them!" General Arnold said angrily, his voice suddenly loud and urgent. "I need them caught, captain. The *president* needs them caught," he added, running a hand distractedly through his hair as he turned away from her, wracking his brain for a solution.

Unsure if the discussion was at an end, Captain Cornwallis stood uncomfortably, not knowing whether to stay or to leave the general to his thoughts. As she waited nervously, she unconsciously patted her holstered gun, a habit that calmed her whenever she felt anxious or unsure.

General Arnold looked at her again and saw her weapon. His eyes narrowed.

"Wait. Are any of our guns unaccounted for?"

"Umm ... yes," the captain replied. "Three of the Mark 2 laser pistols, I think."

"But doesn't the Mark 2 have a trackable chip?"

"Umm ... yes, General. I believe so."

"And didn't one of the Regs report that at least one civilian was armed and returned fire outside the school?"

"Yes, sir. That is, I think so, sir."

"Then have the weapons traced immediately. If my hunch is correct, it should lead us straight to them."

"Yes, sir!" she replied. "Should we send in the helicopters, General?"

"No, captain. Ground troops only. I want your top Fixers ready to go within fifteen minutes," he said.

As the captain rushed off to instruct her team, General Arnold smiled grimly to himself. Soon he would have Locke and the others in his clutches again. And this time, there would be no escape.

5 | Locke's Mistake

"So how do we do this broadcast?" Sol asked. "Do you still have your gear?"

"No," Locke replied, shaking his head. "It was at a safe house I had here in town. But Arnold knows all about it. That's where he found Alex and me yesterday. We cannot go back."

"But if he found your gear won't he know what you were planning?' Harriet asked, frowning.

"Possibly, but I don't think so. The equipment I was using is common enough and the computer files are encrypted. He'd have to know exactly what I was thinking of doing and be really looking for it, which I don't think is the case."

"But you don't know for sure?" Alex's dad asked.

"No. It's a risk we'll have to take," Locke conceded.

"Great! What could possibly go wrong?" Iggy asked sarcastically. "So where else can we get access to the technology you need? Do you have it here?" he asked, scanning the cabin's stuffed shelves hopefully.

"No. But I think I know where we can find it, or at least get the help we need."

"Where?" asked several voices at once.

"There's a place in the forest about a week's march north of here. A community where people live off-grid, where they rejected the MeChip and live, I believe, in peace and solitude. I have never been there, but I think I can find it."

"Does the government know about it?" asked Tom.

"I don't think so; or if they do, they ignore it. Thousands of people have gone off-grid over the years, carving out a simpler existence in unpopulated forests or other wilderness areas."

"Why doesn't the government round them all up?" Alex asked, curious.

"Why bother if they're not a threat to their control? Off-gridders just want to be left alone; the government has no reason to waste time and resources on them."

"So that's the plan?" Iggy asked impatiently. "We head north and try to find this town, this ... what's it called?

"Hope," Locke answered. "The town of Hope."

"Sounds alright to me," Alex said as the others nodded. "What are we waiting for?"

They began preparing immediately, Locke handing out backpacks they filled with as much gear as they could carry: from tents to water bottles, food to blankets, flashlights, bear and bug spray, and even the two hunting rifles and the bow and arrows. Within thirty minutes, they were ready.

"There's one thing been worrying me, Dr. L.," Tom said as they stood outside in the wan morning sunlight waiting for Locke to secure the outer door.

"What's that?" Locke called over his shoulder.

"Why can't the Regs find us here? I mean, don't they have some technology like—I don't know—infrared heat-seeking radars or satellites or something?"

"I don't believe so. Almost all their investment has been in microchip technology like the MeChip. After all, it has been their best method of controlling people for many years. What else do they need?"

"So with our MeChips broken we're untraceable?" Tom asked.

"Unless we have something else with a trackable chip in it," Locke said. "Now, if we're all ready, shall we depart? This way please," he said, leading them around the edge of the low cliff face.

"Who cares if they can find us? Even if they do, we've got these," Iggy said, holding up his Mark 2 laser pistol.

"What did you say?" Locke asked, spinning around.

"I said we've got these," Iggy declared, still brandishing his gun for all to see.

"Oh no," Locke whispered, putting a hand to his mouth.

"What's wrong?" Abby asked. "Are you alright, Dr. Locke?"

"I am afraid not, my dear. In fact, I've made a terrible mistake," he said, eyeing Iggy's pistol in dismay.

6 | Iggy's Aim

"**I** said we'll do it!" Iggy insisted, shouting down the others as his friend Frank nodded his agreement. "Listen, Frank and I are the fittest and the fastest here. We're on the school football team, for smeck's sake! Now give us the other guns," he ordered, looking at Alex and Locke.

"Fine," said Locke at last. "But it should be me doing this. It was my mistake after all. I should have remembered last night that the Fixers' new weapons have a chip in them."

"Listen, when you can run 40 yards in 4.5 seconds, you can take the mission, alright old man?" Iggy said dismissively as Locke handed Frank his gun.

"Very well," Locke sighed.

"And you," Iggy said, turning to Alex. "Hand it over."

There was silence for a moment as Alex looked at Iggy, thinking hard.

"I don't think so, Iggy," he said at last.

"Why not?

"Because I'm going with you."

"No!" said several voices at once.

"Why? We don't need you. Frank and I have got this," Iggy said dismissively.

"Iggy's right," Locke said firmly as Alex's mom and dad nodded their agreement.

"I don't care. I'm going, too," Alex repeated, now determined to join the mission.

"No way. We don't need a skinny little dexter like you," Iggy said, looking at Alex and shaking his head. "You'll only slow us down."

"Not true. You're forgetting I made the track team last year. I won the 5k, remember?"

"But we don't need you," Iggy insisted, sounding annoyed.

"Iggy's right. Why do you want to go with them, Alex?" his mom asked, rubbing her injured hand anxiously.

"Because ... because ... I just think three of us will have more chance of success than two."

"Secrecy is the key, Alex," Locke said. "The more of you there are, the more chance of being spotted."

"Yes, but if they're already on our trail and we need to fight, then three is better than two," Alex replied, sticking to his guns. "And if they are following us, then we need to leave now."

"But—"

"I'm not changing my mind," Alex insisted angrily. "We'll be back soon, anyway. Come on, let's go," he said, handing his X-shaped guitar to Tom and walking quickly away from the group before anyone could object.

Iggy and Frank caught up with him moments later.

"What did you do that for, dexter?" Frank said, looking down at Alex as they made their way past trees and bushes.

"Trying to be the center of attention again, huh?" Iggy added, shaking his head.

"No. I just think I can help, is all," Alex replied defensively.

"You're the only one who does," Iggy said scathingly. "Well, if you're going to come with us, just do as I say, alright?" he added as they reached the edge of the forest.

As Iggy and Frank brushed past Alex and began to lead the way, Alex wondered to himself exactly why he *had* decided to come along. The truth was, he didn't really want to do this mission at all. But something was gnawing at him—a feeling that he couldn't quite trust

Iggy. Not with this task. And definitely not with the guns. After all, hadn't Iggy been in contact with Slade Arnold and almost stopped Alex performing last night? And even if Iggy had helped him by knocking out Arnold in the auditorium, did that mean they could really depend on him? Alex wasn't so sure. No, it was better if he tagged along to make sure Iggy and his sidekick Frank did the job right.

Iggy led them cautiously out of the thinning trees and into a field. It had a single tree in the middle and led steeply down towards the edge of town. Alex guessed it might once have been a pasture for cows or sheep, but now it was empty of livestock and overgrown with weeds and bushes. The light was brighter here than in the forest, although dark clouds were gathering overhead, shadowing the sun.

Iggy navigated his way downhill, moving slowly and staying among the higher grass and bushes in an attempt to stay concealed. Frank followed with Alex in the rear.

The plan was simple enough. They would sneak down the hill and hide by the road that skirted the edge of town, wait for passing trucks or pickups, then toss the guns in the back. That way, anyone tracking the weapons would follow the vehicles, throwing them off the scent completely. They would then return to the woods and meet by a particularly tall tree near the forest's edge.

The first part of the plan went perfectly. Iggy guided them down the hill seemingly unseen and they found a small clump of stunted trees by the roadside. A steady stream of vehicles was passing in both directions. The first few were cars, which was no help at all. Finally, they saw an old open-topped truck trundling towards them.

"Frank, give me your gun," Iggy ordered, holding out his hand.

"Why should you get to throw it?" Frank asked, looking affronted. "Why can't I do it?"

"Because I'm the smeckin' quarterback. It's what I do!" Iggy replied derisively as he snatched the firearm from his friend.

As the truck passed, Iggy took aim and lofted the gun into the air. It arced gracefully towards the back of the truck, landing perfectly on top of its load of potatoes. Then the vehicle was gone, receding into the distance with its extra cargo, fumes spewing from its exhaust.

Despite himself, Alex was impressed. Iggy really had a good arm.

"See, Franklin, I told you we didn't need you. This is easy," Iggy announced in his usual arrogant drawl.

And that was when the shot struck.

7 | Carnage

The laser beam scythed between Iggy and Alex, smashing the tree behind them and sending splinters spitting in every direction. Alex looked up in shock and saw several Fixers just up the hill, aiming at them from behind the bushes.

"Down!" yelled Alex as he leaped to one side, scrambling behind another tree as more shots struck all around. He looked to his left and saw Iggy had done the same and was already concealed behind another tree. Not only that, but the older boy was already returning fire, kneeling and aiming his gun carefully at their attackers. As Alex watched, one of the Fixers screamed and fell backwards as Iggy's shot found its mark, striking the sinister figure in the chest. Alex joined in, catching another Fixer in the shoulder with his shot and sending him sprawling to the ground.

But Frank had no gun. Panicked, he left the shelter of the trees and began to sprint along the side of the road, looking desperately for a gap in the traffic. He darted onto the road but a laser blast caught him in the back, smashing him across the median line and into the path of an oncoming car.

The vehicle tried to swerve away, its brakes screeching as it crossed the center line ... too late! With a sickening crunch, Frank went flying onto the windshield and then over the roof, falling out of sight and onto the road behind. Other vehicles slammed on brakes to avoid the collision. Some sent dust pluming into the air as they skidded off the road. The car that had hit Frank smashed into a pickup truck, which in turn was rear-ended by another vehicle as the jarring screech of metal-on-metal rent the air. For a moment, the Fixers' attack slackened as they, too, were distracted by the pile-up. Iggy stood rooted to the spot, unable to look away from the carnage, from the place his friend had been struck.

"Come on!" Alex shouted, pulling Iggy towards the road as they zigzagged between the stationary vehicles. Together they sprinted to the other side of the street, ducking low to avoid any further shots as they dashed to where they had seen Frank fall.

He was lying on his back by the side of the road. His eyes were closed and his limbs were splayed out at odd angles. There was a dark crimson patch spreading slowly on the gravel beneath his head. There was no sign of life; no movement, no rise-and-fall of his chest to show he was still breathing. Nothing. For a few seconds, the two teenagers simply stood and stared at Frank's lifeless form. Then a siren began to blare in the distance, jerking Alex back to life.

"Iggy, we can't do anything for him. We need to go," Alex said quietly.

But Iggy ignored him. He was still staring at his friend, motionless, a look of incomprehension on his face.

"Iggy, we need to go," Alex said again, more urgently this time.

There was a movement behind them and they turned to see a Fixer emerge from behind a car, face hidden by his dark, wide-brimmed hat, long black coat billowing as he ran. The Fixer saw them, and quickly raised his gun.

Alex lifted his weapon, knowing in that millisec he would be too slow, knowing he wouldn't fire in time.

He was right. His gun was still in motion as the beam lanced out.

But it was not the Fixer who was first to fire.

It was Iggy.

Faster than Alex would have thought humanly possible, he whipped up his weapon and let loose a single blast. It struck the Fixer on the side of his head and he fell backwards, landing heavily by a stationary car. Alex saw the elderly man behind the wheel, his eyes wide with shock at what he'd just witnessed. But there was no time to worry about him, no time to worry about anyone as a second Fixer rushed from behind the line of vehicles, saw Alex and Iggy, and tried to aim his weapon.

Once more Iggy was too fast. Frighteningly fast. He let loose one shot, then another. The first flew inches wide of the mark, but the second struck their foe full in the body. The man dropped his weapon and clutched at his stomach, then crumpled to the ground.

"Come on, we have to get out of here," Alex said, urging Iggy to escape. Together, they sprinted down the far side of the road, passing the ever-growing line of vehicles now joining the gridlock. Alex had to strain to keep up with Iggy's blistering pace as the older boy surged ahead.

They had darted the length of three football fields, perhaps four, before Iggy finally slowed down, then stopped. They were still by the side of the road but had now left the traffic jam behind, although more vehicles continued to pass them by, their drivers unaware they were about to find the street blocked.

"Where do you think we should—" Alex began, but Iggy interrupted him.

"What the smeck was that?" Iggy said accusingly, stepping forward and jabbing a finger into Alex's chest.

"What was what?" Alex replied, utterly confused.

"I thought you said you could help us. You were useless back there. Useless! And now Frank's ... Frank's ..." Iggy tailed off before turning away. Alex saw him run a hand across his eyes.

Alex didn't know what to say. He realized, dimly, that they were probably both in shock. Taking a deep breath to calm himself, he decided their first task was to escape. After that, they could get rid of the guns and try to circle back towards the forest. He was about to suggest this when he noticed a black SUV approaching. Rather than carrying on towards the line of vehicles up ahead, it braked sharply and pulled over onto the curbside barely twenty paces from them, sending gravel spinning into the air as it slid to a stop.

For a moment nothing happened. Alex and Iggy stared at the vehicle, Alex holding his gun tightly as he strained to see the shadowed shape obscured behind the dark-tinted windows.

He gasped as the driver's door opened and a man in a dark greatcoat emerged. He was stocky and powerfully built. His hair was cut short, brown but flecked with gray. His face was impassive as he looked at them from hooded blue eyes.

It was General Arnold.

8 | Arnold's Offer

No one spoke. Alex stared at their enemy as he stood motionless, arms folded across his broad chest. Finally, the general broke the silence.

"Good morning, boys. I'm delighted to see you. I hope you've come here to turn yourselves in?" His tone was courteous, almost friendly.

"No way. I'll never surrender!" Alex shouted back.

"How very predictable, Franklin. And how about you, Iggy? Will you return to the right side? You have done good work for me these past few weeks. I know you almost stopped this renegade from playing his little song last night when you fought with him backstage. There is no need for you to be punished if you join me now. In fact, you will be rewarded for your service." General Arnold's manner was amiable and polite. Once more, Alex detected the faintest trace of an unfamiliar accent. What was it? English, perhaps? But that didn't matter right now.

Alex turned to look at Iggy. The older boy's brows were knitted and his forehead corrugated as if in the grip of some great internal turmoil. He rubbed a hand across his eyes, still staring at Slade Arnold as if hypnotized. Very hesitantly, as if unsure of himself, he took a step towards their adversary.

"What are you doing?" Alex said, grabbing his arm. "You can't possibly be thinking of joining him. This man tortured Locke. He tortured Abby, for smeck's sake. And his thugs just killed Frank!"

Iggy stopped. He looked at Alex as if he'd been doused in cold water, shook his head, and turned towards General Arnold, eyes blazing.

"Alex is right. How could you do those things? I trusted you, General. I trusted you!" He was shouting now, the spell shattered as he fixed his gaze on Slade Arnold.

"Don't listen to the boy," Arnold replied dismissively. "There are always casualties in war, Iggy. But I can protect you, teach you. Don't choose the wrong side," he said, his voice dropping so low Alex had to strain to hear him.

"I know what side I'm on and it's not yours, you smeckin' lunatic. I wish I'd hit you harder last night," Iggy shot back angrily.

"So it was you who gave me this memento of the evening's events?" Arnold said and he sounded almost amused as he rubbed the back of his head. "All will be forgiven if you give yourself up to me now. Hand me your weapon and no one will be hurt."

This seemed to anger Iggy even more. He pointed his gun at Arnold who stood impassively, arms still crossed, an odd smile now playing across his lips.

"Go ahead," he said quietly.

For a long moment, Iggy and the general stared at each other, the gun still aimed at Arnold's chest. Alex held his breath, unsure what to do, unsure what he *wanted* to happen next.

There was a distant shout and Iggy and Alex whirled around. Several Fizers had emerged from among the gridlocked traffic and were running in their direction. They were no more than 100 yards away.

"Come on, we have to get out of here," Alex urged, pulling once more on Iggy's arm.

Iggy nodded, took one last look at General Arnold, and turned to run.

"You're making a big mistake," came the general's voice as the two of them sprinted away from the unmoving figure, his arms still crossed as he watched them flee the scene.

9 | Iggy's Hood

Iggy led them off the road. Instead of heading towards the forest, however, he sprinted in the opposite direction and towards the town, rushing down the nearest street before taking a left turn, then a right as Alex struggled to keep up.

"Where are we going?" Alex panted as Iggy paused on a street corner to let a car pass.

Iggy didn't reply but instead took off once more, leading Alex deeper into town, keeping up a relentless pace and never pausing except where traffic blocked their way. Finally, after ten more minutes of hard running Iggy slowed down, then stopped.

Alex caught up with him and looked around. There was no sign of pursuit. At least, not yet.

"Where are we?" Alex asked, panting and looking around uncertainly.

"My 'hood," Iggy muttered. "I live here. Correction—*used to* live here."

"You live here? With your parents?" Alex asked.

"Just my mom. I never knew my dad," Iggy replied matter-of-factly.

"Oh, right," Alex replied, feeling strangely embarrassed. Why hadn't he known Iggy only had a mom? Single-parent families were really uncommon in Lincoln. How come no one had told him?

They were silent for a moment. Alex still felt awkward and ill at ease, but if Iggy noticed he showed no sign. Instead, the older boy was busy looking up and down the quiet street, obviously alert to signs of pursuit.

"Smeck, this place is a dump," he said finally, frowning.

Iggy was right. Without the MeChip's rose-tinted view, Iggy's old neighborhood looked squalid. The roads were pockmarked and trash-strewn, the apartment blocks had a neglected, uncared-for air, shopfronts wore a layer of dirt and grime on windows and awnings, while the few people passing by looked ailing and careworn. The air swirled with smog as the twin towers of Bright Green Mining belched out their filth under an angry gray sky.

"Can you believe I actually thought my neighborhood was *uber* cool?" Iggy asked, wrinkling his nose in disgust at the sights and smells. "That MeChip sure did a smeckin' number on us, huh?"

Alex nodded, unsure how to respond to Iggy's odd mood. He was feeling shaken and disoriented from what had happened with General Arnold and the Fixers. At what had just happened to Iggy's friend. Trying to keep the image of Frank's broken body out of his mind, Alex turned to face the older boy.

"What are we doing here, Iggy?"

"Isn't it obvious?"

"Not to me," Alex replied, feeling like he must be missing something. "Why did we come into town again?"

"If we'd run back to the forest Arnold would have known where we were going," Iggy replied slowly, as if speaking to a little child. "Our mission is to lose the weapons and help throw him off the scent at the same time. That's why I came here."

"I get that. But why come so far into city? Why not stay on the periphery?" Alex persisted.

"Because I know this neighborhood like the back of my hand," Iggy replied. "I can put the guns somewhere that will send them on the wrong trail without getting us caught."

"What do you mean?"

"Come on; I'll show you."

Iggy led Alex down the street, his eyes flicking left and right. Finally, he seemed to spot something he liked in a back alley. Leading them down it, he motioned for Alex to hide in the shadows of a doorway. Just a few steps away Alex saw a truck parked by a loading bay that led to the back of a store. They waited in silence for several seconds before a balding, burly, middle-aged man emerged from the shop and stepped into the back of the truck. A moment later he staggered out carrying a large box before disappearing into the rear of the building.

"Your gun, quick!" Iggy said, holding out his hand. Feeling strangely reluctant, Alex handed over his weapon and Iggy immediately made his way down the alley, staying close to the shadowed walls. Looking around to make sure the coast was clear, he jumped up into the back of the truck and disappeared from view. A moment later he emerged empty-handed ... just as the man came out of the building.

"Hey, what the smeck are you doing in my vehicle?" the man said loudly, looking at Iggy accusingly.

"Nothing," Iggy said innocently.

"You'd better not have taken anything," he said, stepping forward aggressively.

"I haven't, honest. Look!" Iggy replied, holding up his empty hands and turning out his pockets. "Nothing."

"Well smeck off, then."

Iggy strutted back down the street, then stopped by the doorway where Alex remained hidden, leaning down and pretending to tie a shoelace.

From his hiding place, Alex could see the man still watching Iggy.

"I said smeck off!" said the man. "Shouldn't you be in school or something?"

"I'm going, I'm going," Iggy shouted back over his shoulder before whispering to Alex, "Stay where you are and join me round the corner once he goes inside."

Iggy made his way to the end of the alley and sauntered out of view. The man continued to watch him suspiciously for a few seconds. Finally, he stepped into the back of the truck once more, appearing a moment later with a large crate of beer, which he carried into the shop. After waiting a millisec to be sure the man was gone, Alex rushed around the corner where Iggy was leaning against a rusty lamppost.

"Come on," he said to Alex. Without waiting for an answer, he started off up the street, then took a left turn as Alex struggled to keep up with the taller boy's long stride.

"Did you get rid of them?"

"Of course," Iggy grunted. "Put them right in the back of the truck behind a bunch of boxes."

"But won't they track him down pretty quickly?"

"Who knows?" Iggy shrugged. "But on the side of the truck it says they deliver across the state, so with any luck he'll be back on the freeway soon and lead them to another town or city. And when they finally track him down, the last place they'll have seen us is the town, *not* the forest."

Neither of them spoke. Despite himself, Alex felt impressed at Iggy's actions and quick thinking. Not only had he dispatched two of the Fixers back by the road, he had also got rid of all three guns.

"Where now?" he asked finally.

"You'll see," Iggy answered.

"Not your house?" Alex said, suddenly suspicious.

"I'm not nuts, Franklin!" Iggy shot back. "I know we can't go to my apartment."

"Not the forest either, right?"

"Why not?"

"You said it yourself earlier; we don't want Arnold to know we're in the forest. I think we should hide out awhile in Lincoln, keep our heads down and wait until dusk, then make our way back to the forest under cover of darkness."

"The others might have left our meetup point if we take too long," Iggy warned, frowning.

"True, but unless you know a route back to the forest that makes us invisible, I don't see how we can avoid being seen. They'll be searching for us now. Better to wait for darkness and the hunt to die down." As if proving Alex's point, they heard the sound of a Regs' siren and the blast of a car horn just a couple of blocks away in the direction they were heading. In the distance, Alex could just make out the tell-tale whir of a helicopter's rotor blades.

"Fine," Iggy said after a moment's hesitation.

"Is there somewhere we can hide out?"

"This way," Iggy replied. He led Alex quickly along several more streets until they reached a park. There was an open stretch of lawn with a kids' playground and a statue of Abraham Lincoln in the center. In this miserable, Me-Chipless version of the world, the place had a forlorn and neglected look. The children's climbing frame was covered in rust and the grass was yellowed and strewn with empty candy wrappers and old aluminum cans. A pigeon sat on President Lincoln's head, eyeing the two boys beadily as they passed. Bright Green Mining's enormous towers were just a few blocks away, screening the sky with their relentless fumes.

There was no one else in sight as Iggy led them towards some bushes and a stand of trees at the far end of the park. Pushing through the undergrowth, Alex followed him into a tiny clearing behind the bushes and out of sight. A high wall stood close behind them. It was, Alex had to admit, a good place to hide.

"I'll keep watch first," Alex said, pulling himself up into a small tree and sitting on one of the branches. "One of us should rest."

"Fine by me," Iggy replied, spreading himself out on the ground below and immediately closing his eyes.

Alex kept watch for a couple of hours. He concentrated his thoughts on the present—on watching and listening for signs of pursuit—at the same time trying hard *not* to think about what had just happened to Frank. Eventually he woke Iggy, switching places with the older boy.

The ground was layered with fallen leaves, making it a comfortable place to rest. Alex lay down and closed his eyes, then opened them as the awful scene at the roadside started to replay itself in his mind's eye. He looked up at Iggy, who was now scanning the park from his perch on the branch. His thoughts turned to General Arnold and a wave of anger surged through him.

"Iggy, can I ask you something?" he said at last.

"Sure."

"How long have you known Slade Arnold?"

"Not long," Iggy said finally, frowning. "A few weeks, I think. Maybe longer."

"You don't know?" Alex asked, surprised.

"Listen, dexter, a lot's been happening, okay? I can't remember everything," Iggy snarled.

But that didn't sound right to Alex.

"I wonder if losing our MeChips is messing up our memories?" Alex asked, as much to himself as to Iggy. "I'm a bit hazy on some stuff, too. And I'm starting to remember things I never have before," he said, recalling a thought he'd had when he'd woken up that morning. But had that been a memory, or just a dream? Surely it couldn't be true. Could it? He hoped desperately that it wasn't.

Luckily, Iggy didn't seem interested in Alex's memories, apparently lost in his own. Silence fell between them and Alex lay back and closed his eyes again. He thought of Abby. What was the loss of the MeChip doing to *her* memories? Had she recalled what had happened in the tree house? Or did she still think she was dating Iggy? And what about her father? Did she know what had really taken place just a few weeks ago on that terrible night after he'd coughed up blood at the barbecue? Alex's thoughts drifted to his parents, to John Locke, to his friends Tom and Sol, and finally to last night and his performance at the Best Band contest. There was just so much to process. Too much. He felt so tired, not just physically but emotionally, too, as he lay back on the soft leaves …

He opened his eyes with a start. It took him a millisec to remember where he was. How long had he slept? He noticed the light was different, brighter now and dappling through the trees from another direction. As he lay among the fallen leaves, his eyes scanned the branches for Iggy. There was no sign of him. Where could he be?

He was about to call out when he heard a voice close by.

"I'll check now."

Alex froze. As he lay there, prone and vulnerable, he heard a rustling in the bushes. The muzzle of a gun pushed through the foliage, followed an instant later by a hand and an arm almost directly above him.

As Alex watched, horror-struck, a face appeared. He could see the man's eyes scanning left and right, glancing up into the trees. The man was wearing a black, peaked cap with a silver eagle button on the front. It was a Regulator.

10 | Regs and Riddles

Alex stared, frozen in place, at the man above him. He heard a noise near his ear and out of the corner of his eye saw something black appear at ground level. The Reg's leather boot was just inches from Alex's face.

So this was it, then. The Reg just needed to look down and he'd see Alex. He was so close Alex could make out the individual hairs in the man's reddish-brown mustache, the small mole on his chin. But Alex could do nothing to save himself. He felt rooted to the ground as he lay there defenseless, unable to move a muscle.

And this, perhaps, is what saved him.

"Anything back there?" came a voice from further away.

"No," the Reg shouted back. "Just some trees and a wall."

A moment later the gun and head withdrew and Alex heard the crack of twigs and the rustling of foliage being brushed aside as the Reg retreated the way he'd come.

Alex did not move for a long time. He simply lay there waiting for his heart to stop pounding against his ribs, for the sound of the Regs to recede.

Later, much later, he got up, quietly climbed the nearest tree, and looked out on the park. The place was empty once more. No Regs ... no one at all.

How had that man not seen him? He had only to look down, thought Alex, glancing at the spot where he'd been just moments before. It was cast in shadow. Had that helped? Probably it was that—and his paralyzing fear—which had rendered him motionless and harder to see. But why had he, Alex, frozen yet again? A feeling of shame washed over him.

From his concealed perch on the branch, Alex saw a mother appear. She was pushing a toddler in a stroller while a second child, this one a little older, ran around her legs, playing some sort of game, her laughter punctuated by little coughing fits the mother didn't seem to notice. But they didn't stop, carrying on along the path and soon disappearing from view.

Alex sat there trying to ignore the little voice in his head whispering that Iggy would have done better than him. Iggy wouldn't have frozen, said the voice. But where was Iggy? Alex thought once again about General Arnold and how he'd been using Iggy. Was Iggy really on their side? Could Alex trust him?

His thoughts were interrupted by a sound from behind. Whipping his head around Alex saw a hand appear at the top of the wall, then an arm as someone pulled themselves up from the other side. A millisec later, Iggy's face appeared, followed by a boot as he hauled himself onto the top of the wall. He, too, scanned the small clearing, saw Alex in the tree and nodded, then vaulted down, landing lightly on the carpet of leaves and dirt.

"You're awake, then, sleeping beauty," Iggy said. "Here you are." He threw something up to Alex, who caught it without thinking and looked at it in surprise.

"What's this?"

"It's a blueberry muffin, dexter."

"But where did you get it from?"

"There's a bakery near here."

"So you just walked into a shop?" Alex asked, incredulous that Iggy should have risked capture for a bit of food.

"Of course not. I used to work there on weekends. They toss their old pastries in the trash out the back around 4 p.m. I figured we should try to eat, so I hid behind the dumpster and waited. I got loads of stuff—look." He held out a large plastic bag filled with food.

"Oh ... great," Alex said.

"Aren't you going to eat it?" Iggy asked, raising an eyebrow.

"Oh, yeah," Alex replied, biting half-heartedly into the muffin. After the shock he'd just had he felt sick rather than hungry.

"Jeez, you could try sounding a bit more grateful. They're better than Locke's crappy cookies."

"Oh, no, it's great. It's just ... the Regs were here."

"Here?"

"Yes. One of them looked into the clearing but didn't see me. I'm not sure how," Alex said, trying to keep his voice level.

"Right," Iggy said slowly, clearly thinking. "They'll still be looking for us, won't they? But like you said, the longer we wait the more the hunt's likely to die down or go someplace else. Once it's dark we can try sneaking out of here."

Iggy climbed a nearby tree and started munching on a muffin, watching the park in silence. Eventually, Alex spoke.

"Iggy, why did you help General Arnold?"

"Eh? What? Oh, that. Well, he told me you were doing something you shouldn't. He said you were caught up in things you didn't understand and I should keep an eye on you."

"And you believed him?"

"Why not? You always were a gullible dexter, Franklin."

"Then why did you help us in the end? Why did you hit him?" Alex asked, ignoring the insult.

"When my MeChip broke I realized he was lying. I'm not sure why. It's not like I remembered anything special. But I just knew. Besides, I could see he'd taken Abby prisoner. No one does that to my girl."

Alex felt an almost irresistible urge to shout at Iggy; to tell him Abby wasn't *his* girl, that his memory and his MeChip had played him false. But this was not the time for arguments so he kept his tongue. Silence fell again as both boys sank inside themselves and their thoughts.

Meanwhile, dusk had fallen. Below them, the odd commuter wandered through the park and a couple of kids stopped by the climbing frame for a few minutes, chattering animatedly about something or other. But no one stayed for long. Above them, clouds gathered once more, while the smog from the twin towers seemed to thicken, swirling ever closer and enveloping them like a blanket. Alex coughed as he inhaled the dirty air. Had it always been like this? Or had it gotten worse as the years passed? Because of his MeChip's endless lies, he would probably never know. Meanwhile, the poor people still living in ignorance under the MeChip's control had to breathe this in every day and night. Alex felt a surge of anger and disgust at the people who had done this—at General Arnold and President Davison and all the rest.

"Come on," he said suddenly, still fuming to himself as he rose to his feet. "It's dark enough. We should go." Instantly, Iggy climbed down the tree as the two of them left their hiding place and went out into the night.

11 | Barbed Wire

It was easier than Alex expected. Iggy led them down the side alleys and backstreets of his old neighborhood, through a disused warehouse, and past an old apartment block that looked deserted, the moonlight catching on the windows' broken shards and jagged edges. Several times Regs' SUVs appeared and shot around the corner towards them, sirens blazing, as Iggy and Alex were forced to hide, ducking behind dumpsters and parked cars. But they weren't spotted and the Regs whisked away and off into the night, lights still flashing, alarms screaming. Alex was sure their efforts to escape were assisted by the smog, which made it hard to see more than twenty yards in front of them. Not only that, but half the street lamps weren't working.

Soon they left the edge of town, sneaking across the road where they'd spoken with General Arnold and up into the fields on the other side. It took some time in the darkness to find the tree they were looking for, but once they had climbed the hill and emerged from the city smog it became easier even with passing clouds obscuring the moon's light. Finally, Alex spotted the tallest tree and they made their way cautiously towards it. Would the others still be there?

It wasn't until they were standing directly beneath it that they saw the shapes.

"Put your hands above your heads and don't move. We're armed," hissed a voice out of the darkness.

"Who's that?" Iggy replied, ignoring the threats. "Is that you, Locke?"

"No, it's Ben," came the reply, surprise in his voice.

"Dad?" said Alex, rushing forward. A moment later he was being embraced by not just his dad but his mom, too. He breathed a huge sigh of relief and for a long time just held the two of them. When he finally pulled away, he overheard Iggy and his mom, Alice, talking.

"But where's Frank?" Alice asked.

"He ... didn't make it," Iggy replied quietly.

"What do you mean? What happened?" Alice asked with a note of panic in her voice.

"Where are the others?" Iggy asked. "I only want to say this once." His voice sounded odd, strained and higher pitched than usual.

"They're waiting a little further into the forest. This way," said Alex's dad.

They soon emerged into a small clearing. As the moonlight broke from behind a passing cloud Alex saw the shapes of several people sitting or standing, and the bulkier outline of four small tents.

"Who's there?" came a voice Alex knew was Locke's.

"It's us, John," said Alex's mom. "And we've got Iggy and Alex."

The others stepped forward to welcome them. Sol patted Alex on the back and Tom took him in a bearhug, whispering "Glad you're back, dude."

As Tom stepped back Alex saw Abby. She was looking from Alex to Iggy and back again. For a moment, nobody spoke. Before Alex could act, however, Iggy moved towards her.

"Relax, Abby, I'm fine, no need to worry," he said as he leaned in to hug her, the bravado back in his voice again. Alex felt a surge of anger but with an effort managed to control himself. It was not the right time to have this conversation, he told himself.

"But where's Frank?" Iggy's mom asked again. "And why did you take so long? We've been worried sick about you."

So Iggy told them. He explained everything, from beginning to end, faltering only at the part where Frank was shot by the Fixer and hit by the car. At that point Alex spoke up, relating as quickly as he could what had happened while trying not to let the image of Frank's broken body steal back into his brain.

After that, Iggy took up the story once more. To Alex's immense relief, Iggy didn't criticize Alex's actions or try to belittle him. He just told it straight, sticking to the facts, apparently keen to get it over with.

When Iggy was finished no one spoke for at least a minute, the silence broken only by quiet sobs from Iggy's mom, whom Alex guessed had known Frank pretty well since he was one of Iggy's best friends. Finally, John Locke spoke up.

"Iggy, I'm sorry to have to ask, but I have one more question for you. It's about Slade Arnold." Iggy didn't reply, so Locke went on.

"Are you sure he didn't do more to try to stop you escaping?"

"No, I told you, he just tried to talk me into staying ... *us* into staying, I guess. Then we ran off."

"And you didn't hear signs of pursuit?"

"I told you, he didn't follow us. He just stood there."

"You're sure he didn't shoot at you as you ran?"

"No. I'm not sure he even had a gun."

"But—"

"Listen, old man, I've said everything I'm going to say about it, alright? Now, can we just drop it?"

There was another silence, this time broken by Iggy himself.

"Hey, who wants a pastry? They're a bit stale, but still pretty good," he said, handing the bag to Locke before striding away from the group and over to the far side of the clearing, where he sat on a fallen tree. After a moment his mother followed him, sitting beside him and placing an arm around his shoulders. Snatches of their whispered conversation carried in the air as the rest of them stood in silence, but the wind in the trees made it impossible to tell what they were talking about.

"Are you alright, Alex?" came a voice from close by. Alex turned and saw Abby, her face shadowed in the moonlight.

"Not really. You?"

"No. But I'm glad you're back."

She opened her mouth to speak again when Locke interrupted.

"We should all try to sleep. We're starting a long journey tomorrow. We'll take shifts in standing guard. I'll go first, then Tom, Sol, Ben, and finally Liz," he said, nodding at Alex's mom and dad.

As Alex climbed into the tent and lay down near Tom and Sol, shivering a little from the cold, his last thought before he fell asleep was about Locke's question to Iggy. Locke was definitely onto something, Alex realized. Why *had* General Arnold not tried harder to stop them escaping? If Arnold had a gun he could have shot at them the millisec Iggy dropped his guard and turned to run. Arnold looked pretty fit, too. If he didn't have a weapon, why didn't he give chase? And why was Iggy so reluctant to talk about it? Did he know more about it than he was letting on? Something about Arnold's actions just didn't add up.

They walked a long way the following day. Despite everything, Alex had slept well that night and felt in a lighter mood as they prepared to set out. Spreading out an old-fashioned paper map on the leaf-covered ground, Locke had shown them the path they'd need to take through the forest and explained that it should take about a week—assuming they were lucky and his information about the town of Hope was correct. Having packed up their gear the group set out, with Locke leading them deeper into the forest while referring occasionally to the map and, much more frequently, an old compass.

Alex had been keen to talk more with Abby but she'd attached herself early on to Locke, with whom she seemed to have developed a connection. Alex wondered if the events of two days before, when Locke and Abby had both been captured and tortured by Arnold, had created a bond between them. She walked at the front with him and her mom Susanna, talking animatedly.

Sol, Tom, and Harriet had joined Alex and his parents in the middle of the group, and he had to repeat everything he knew—from his first suspicions and early encounters with Locke to the events of the past two days—at least twice before they were satisfied. The only details he left out were those relating to Abby, especially what happened with their "date" and to her father all those weeks ago. Somehow, he still didn't feel he had the energy or emotional strength to bring them up yet.

Behind them, Iggy, his mom Alice, and Sybil brought up the rear. Alex occasionally caught snatches of their conversation, which seemed to be mostly Alice trying to comfort and calm Sybil, who still seemed in a state of shock.

After an hour or two, though, the talk subsided as fatigue began to set in. Hiking through a forest was no joke, Alex realized, as the rough terrain, bushes, and branches made it impossible to move quickly. While Locke soon located an old track that made the going a little easier, the path was leading them upwards as they went deeper into the hills, with only a few flat areas punctuating the climb. All conversation eventually ceased as they focused on just putting one foot in front of the other.

Breathing heavily, Alex looked behind him and saw Iggy walking in silence. He was staring over Alex's shoulder in Abby's direction, but when he saw Alex looking at him he muttered "What, dexter?" and Alex looked away, at the same time shifting the strap of his guitar, which was cutting into his shoulder. Iggy looked the least tired of anyone in spite of his heavy backpack and gun, Alex thought grudgingly.

Of course, Iggy *had* insisted on having one of the hunting rifles. Still, Alex had to admit Iggy had shown himself more than capable with a weapon during their shoot-out with the Fixers.

Harriet had the other gun as it turned out her family had owned an air rifle and she claimed to be a pretty good shot. Meanwhile, Abby—who was on the school archery team—carried the bow and arrows.

It was late afternoon and the sun was starting to touch the tips of the tallest trees when they hit their first obstacle. As they rounded a bend in the track, Locke, Abby, and Susanna suddenly stopped. Alex and the others soon caught up and saw why.

An old metal gate had been placed across the path. On either side, barbed wire fences disappeared into the trees. A wooden sign was nailed to the fence:

Private Property. Stay Out or Die.

"What do you think, Dr. L.?" Tom asked Locke as the group stared at the message.

"I don't know," Locke said slowly. "The sign looks old. And we need to keep going north, which is where the track leads. But—"

"Then what are we waiting for? Let's keep going," Iggy interrupted.

"Is it worth the risk?" Sol asked, scratching his chin uncertainly.

"Locke said it himself. The sign's old. Look at it!" replied Iggy confidently.

Alex had to agree. The writing was faded. Bleached by the sun and diluted by rain, it had clearly been there a long time.

"There's probably been no one living here for years," Iggy said. "Why waste time trying to find another way around?"

Locke frowned, his forehead corrugated in concern. Finally, he nodded.

"Alright. Let's be careful—"

But Iggy didn't wait. Already he was striding purposefully towards the gate where he began pulling it aside. A millisec later and it was done. The way was clear and open.

"Come on, what are you waiting for?" he said, turning to the others and smiling.

He was still grinning when the first shot rang out.

12 | The Attack

The bullet struck just inches from Iggy's feet, spitting up dust and stones. Fast as ever, Iggy turned and sprinted back the way he'd come, zigzagging to make himself harder to hit.

"Get down! Get off the path," Alex shouted at the others as Iggy rushed towards them

Spurred to action, the group hurried off the track, taking shelter behind trees or crouching behind boulders as a salvo of shots chased them, ricocheting off rocks and splintering trunks.

Alex peered cautiously out from behind a large boulder. It looked like none of them had been hit. He risked a further look towards the gate but could see no one.

Abruptly, the shots ceased. For a moment there was silence. Then a man's voice bellowed at them from the trees up ahead.

"This land belongs to McCullough's Militia. You ain't welcome."

"We wish you no harm. We just wish to pass along the track," Locke yelled back.

"You ain't welcome here. You've had one warning, which is more'n you deserve."

"But we just wish to pass through."

"Turn back now or you'll regret it."

To Alex's great alarm, he saw Locke stand up and step back onto the track, his hands above his head.

"Could I just talk with you for a moment? Look ... I come unarmed and in peace."

There was silence for a moment and Alex thought he heard whispered conversation from the trees near the gate. Finally, another voice spoke up, this one deeper and more commanding.

"You have five seconds to run, old man. Then I shoot to kill."

"But—"

"Five!"

"Please just let me—"

"Four!"

"Don't do this—"

"Three!"

It was no use. Locke turned and ran back to the group, dropping down behind a boulder next to Alex as another volley of shots rang out.

"We're going! Do you hear me, we're going!" Alex shouted at the unseen attackers as Locke panted for breath beside him.

"We should leave. Right now." Alex led the way as they retraced their route back down the hill, crouching low and staying off the track until they were out of sight of the gate. They continued down the trail for another mile or so before Alex spotted a small clearing among the trees. He led them into it and stopped, satisfied they had put enough distance between themselves and their enemy.

"Thank you for leading us safely away from there," Locke said quietly to Alex, his breath still coming in ragged gasps.

"Of course," Alex nodded, pleased at his mentor's compliment.

"What the smeck was that?" Tom asked, his voice shaking slightly.

"Off-gridders," Locke said, turning to face the others.

"Lunatics, more like!" Iggy spat.

"Dr. Locke, the town we're trying to reach won't be like that, will it?" asked Sybil, eyes wide.

"No. There are many types of people who have chosen to go off-grid and escape the MeChip's clutches. This group seems to be of the more aggressive type—distrustful and wary of strangers, wishing only to be left alone. I believe the folks of Hope take a more optimistic point of view, although I'm sure they have ways of defending themselves if required."

"So what now?" Iggy asked. "Do we go back and teach them a lesson?"

"No!" said several voices at once.

"I think we should get as far away from them as possible," Alice said quietly, looking disapprovingly at her son. "You could have been killed back there, Iggy."

"I agree. We are *not* going back," Locke announced as the others—except for Iggy—nodded their approval. "We will skirt east around the edge of their territory and try to get back in the right direction. Here, let's look at the map," he said, putting down his backpack before reaching inside.

It was late in the evening before Locke called a halt. They had made some progress, retracing their steps back down the hill a little further before turning east and following a small stream. Locke was searching for another trail that would take them northeast and eventually back in the right direction, but in the growing darkness they had either not reached it or missed it entirely. Finally, he called for them to stop and the group began setting up camp in a place where the trees grew less close together.

Since they were only a day's march from Lincoln, Locke didn't want to risk a fire or any sort of light, so they huddled together for warmth in the darkness, finishing the last of the stale pastries Iggy had brought. No one spoke much and soon they started to turn in, climbing into tents and trying to sleep while taking it in turns to keep watch. As Alex lay there listening to Tom and Sol's gentle breathing, he heard wolves howling in the distance. What if there were dangerous creatures like that close by? Or members of the militia tracked them here? He hoped whoever was keeping guard would be diligent. Finally, dispirited and depressed, he sank into an uneasy sleep filled with strange and disturbing dreams.

Much, much later he awoke with a start. He opened his eyes and sat up, putting a hand up to his sweat-soaked forehead. The others were still asleep but a grayish early morning light was filtering through the sides of the tent. He had just had a horrifying dream involving his parents. At least, he hoped it was a dream because if it was true—if it was something the MeChip had hidden from him—he thought he would go mad.

He was just making up his mind to wake them when the screaming began.

13 | Screams

Alex's heart gave a giant jolt as the earsplitting sound shredded his eardrums. Unzipping the tent at record speed, he clambered through the entrance, turning left and right as he sought the source of the disturbance. As he stood there uncertainly Iggy brushed past him, rifle in hand, looking out among the trees for signs of an attack.

But the screams were coming from another tent: the one Abby, her mom Susanna, Iggy's mom Alice, Sybil, and Harriet were sharing.

Harriet, who had evidently been standing guard, was staring open-mouthed at the tent as the screaming continued. As the others emerged looking disheveled and shocked the shrieks finally stopped, to be replaced by loud sobbing.

"Is everything alright?" Alex asked uncertainly through the canvas.

"I don't know. It's my mom," came Abby's voice from within.

"Do you need help?" Alex persisted.

"I don't know. I don't think so. Give us a minute."

By now everyone was wide awake and standing outside. Sol and Tom looked quizzically at Harriet and Alex, who shrugged, just as confused as the others about what was happening. Finally, Abby, Susanna, Sybil, and Alice came out of their shelter and joined the others. Susanna's eyes were red. She was visibly shaking.

"What's wrong?" asked Locke gently.

"I had a horrible nightmare about my husband John."

"What happened, Susanna?" asked Alex's mom, looking concerned.

"I thought he ... I dreamed he ... wasn't really my husband," she said, looking at the ground.

"It was just a dream, Susanna," said Alice consolingly, putting an arm around her shoulders.

"But that's just it," Susanna said, her voice shaking. "I don't think it was a dream at all. It felt more like a ... a memory. Something I'd just remembered."

"That can't be true, Susanna. You know it can't," Alex's mom Liz said, frowning.

"But it is," Susanna persisted. "I woke up with a very clear memory of a night when people dressed in black came to the house. It was late ... past midnight. I let them in—I couldn't help myself—and they took John away on a stretcher. He had blood on his face and was so pale. They put a blanket over him and then then they ... they replaced him with someone else. And somehow I thought this new man was my husband. But he wasn't and I—" She stopped, unable to continue. Alice put an arm around her shoulders.

There was silence as the group stood and stared, stunned by her story.

"It must have been a dream, Susanna," said Liz again gently, as if trying to coax an upset child back to reason. "I know it seemed real, but—"

"It *was* real!" Susanna insisted, her voice cracking again. "And I'm not the only one who knows about it."

"What do you mean?" asked Liz, her voice almost a whisper, as if she was suddenly afraid of what the answer might be.

"If you doubt me, ask him," she said accusingly as she turned and pointed at Alex. "Ask your son, Liz. Because he knows ... he knows all about it!"

14 | MeChip Memories

Alex's heart raced as Susanna glared at him accusingly.

"Tell them, Alex," she said. "Tell them the truth. And tell me ... *please* tell me I'm not going mad," she said, her voice no longer angry but desperate, pleading.

Alex felt unable to speak. What should he say? For a millisec, he considered denying it. Wouldn't that give Susanna some comfort, shield her from the awful truth that her husband—Abby's father—was dead? Yet the instant the idea occurred to him, he knew he couldn't do it. He must tell the truth, cut through the deceit and confusion sowed by the MeChip and those evil people who wielded its power. However hard it was, he had to be honest. Susanna deserved it. So did Abby.

"It started at your barbecue," he began as he explained to Susanna—to all of them—exactly what he'd seen that day when her husband had coughed up blood and that night when the Fixers had taken him away on a stretcher. He couldn't look at Susanna or Abby while he spoke. It would have been too hard to see their reactions, to see the pain in their eyes. Instead, he stood awkwardly staring at the ground, unable to meet anyone's gaze.

Silence fell as he ended his tale. It was Abby who finally spoke.

"Why didn't you tell us before?" she asked, her voice so quiet he had to strain to hear her.

"I tried," he said. "The next morning, I tried to tell you when I saw him—the imposter, I mean. By the garden fence. Remember?"

Abby frowned and ran a hand across her eyes as if trying to brush away the false memories implanted by the MeChip.

"I think so," she said. "But when I try to remember things from the past my brain feels fuzzy, like—I don't know—my telescope when it's out of focus."

"You freaked out when I told you," Alex said, trying to help her recall the moment. "You said the imposter *was* your dad and asked how I could say something so horrible about him. And *my* dad was there, too. He sent me back to the house and my parents grounded me," he added, turning to look at them.

"*I* remember," Alex's dad said, looking his son in the eyes. "I had no idea what was really going on. I thought you were pranking them. I'm sorry." He held his son's gaze for several seconds before Alex turned back to Abby. But she was looking away into the trees, running her fingers abstractedly through her hair.

"Susanna and Abby, I am so truly sorry for your loss ... sorrier than you know," Locke said, looking at each of them in turn. "I am also sorry to say many of you—perhaps all of you—will begin to remember things that cause you pain," he continued, now turning to the others. "The MeChip has been manipulating your realities for many years now."

"Not you, though," said Iggy, his voice surly and mutinous.

"I'm sorry?"

"You don't have any false memories, do you? Because you never wore a MeChip. You only created the smeckin' thing!" He was staring at the old man with an anger that surprised Alex. Why did Iggy always seem so keen to pick a fight with Dr. Locke?

"Yes, but he was chainstitched by Arnold. We both were," said Abby, coming to Locke's defense.

"That's not the same," Iggy said dismissively.

"How would you know?" she shot back angrily, eyes blazing. "You don't know how it felt, how bad it was."

"But Iggy is right," Locke admitted, his palms held out in a gesture of peace. "I did not have a MeChip implant for many years and I will never forgive myself for what I did when I created it or for standing by while it was misused. I can only do my best to make amends now and hope—"

"It's too late now, Locke! Whatever happens now you can't undo all the damage you've caused. You never will. Arnold was right about you, you smeckin' old dexter!" Iggy cut in, yelling now.

"Iggy!" his mom Alice said, looking scandalized. "You mind your language, young man! Now apologize."

"No way," Iggy fired back.

"And what exactly did Slade Arnold say to you, Iggy?" Locke asked, raising an eyebrow.

"He ... I ... it's none of your smeckin' business," Iggy replied before turning and striding off into the trees.

"I'm sorry," Alice said to Locke. "My son has a lot of energy ... a lot of anger." Then she, too, turned and ran after her son. A few seconds later they were both lost from view, swallowed by the forest.

There was another lengthy silence as the stunned group looked at one another, trying to process what had just happened.

"Are you alright, John?" Liz asked.

"I'll be fine, Liz," Locke said, trying to smile. "This is hard on all of us. So much change, so much bad news in such a short space of time. It's natural that tempers will fray."

"And you said we may all have flashbacks; memories of things the MeChip hid from us?" asked Alex's dad, frowning.

"I am afraid so, Ben," Locke answered. "But if this happens to you—or any of us—I urge you not to keep these memories to yourselves. Whatever the truth, there is no shame in it. We can and should help each other get through this."

The others nodded. Abby and Susanna were hugging, both in tears, while Alex's own parents were holding hands and Sybil and Harriet had their arms around each other's shoulders. Tom and Sol, meanwhile, were both frowning and looking uncomfortable, while Locke looked weary and older than ever, the lines across his forehead more deeply etched than before, his eyes red and shadowed.

So there were more secrets to be revealed, Alex thought dejectedly. But whose would be next?

15 | The Tower

Four more days passed. Long days of walking deeper and deeper into the forest, higher and higher among the ever-ascending line of hills towards the distant, snow-capped mountains.

While nothing terrible happened—and no secrets were revealed—things were not easy. Locke eventually succeeded in finding the second trail, which was certainly good news. Without it, Alex was convinced they would have become hopelessly lost. Even as it was, the going was tough as the rough path led ever upwards, making it hard even for the fittest among them. Fatigued by long days of hiking and nights camping in unknown places, no one seemed to have much energy to spare for conversation as they trudged their way northwards.

Iggy had rejoined the group a few minutes after his row with Locke without an apology to anyone, acting as if it had never happened. He walked at the rear with his mom and with Sybil, who seemed to have formed a friendship with them. Whatever Alice and Iggy were doing to cheer Sybil up was clearly working, for she seemed more animated and happier than before. Iggy even managed to make her laugh a few times.

Much to Alex's relief, Iggy and Abby didn't seem to be talking much after the argument with Locke, and a frostiness seemed to have settled over the pair. However, to Alex's dismay Abby wasn't being any warmer towards him. He had tried to talk with her a few times but had been rebuffed with short answers and a cold, distant look. He wondered if she blamed him, somehow, for what had happened to her dad. Had he not tried hard enough to explain the truth to her that Sunday morning all those weeks ago? But she'd had the MeChip influencing her then. How could he have persuaded her?

Abby spent most of her time with Locke and her mom at the front of the group, sometimes in silence, sometimes talking quietly in undertones that didn't carry far enough for Alex to hear what was said.

Alex's mom and dad seemed to have grown closer, too, and they spent much of the time walking in silence or talking quietly together. At one point on the second day, Alex wondered if they were arguing, for he saw his father shake his head vigorously, mutter something in an angry undertone, and then glance back at Alex. But whatever was going on was soon sorted out, for a few minutes later Alex saw him take her by the hand, while she rested her head on his shoulder. Meanwhile, the two bass guitarists, Sol and Harriet, had evidently struck up a friendship, leaving Alex with Tom for company.

Usually, Alex would have enjoyed spending time with Tom, who was often funny and—along with Sol—his best friend. Alex had wondered if Tom would want to talk about his parents and his worries about their wellbeing. After all, Tom's mom and dad had both been at the Best Band contest but had been separated from their son in the chaos caused by the Regs and Fixers. Was Tom fearful for their safety?

But Tom had turned inwards since that evening's awful events. He seemed absorbed in some internal mental struggle, although whether it was his parents or some other matter on his mind, Alex couldn't tell. A few times Tom appeared on the verge of sharing something with Alex before apparently thinking better of it. Alex didn't want to push him, but he was surprised at the reluctance of Tom—who liked to talk about *everything*—to confide in him.

When Tom did speak it was mostly to complain that Iggy was monopolizing Sybil. "I thought he was dating Abby? Why doesn't he get back to her, huh?" he grumbled at least a dozen times a day. But Alex just shrugged, unwilling to get into the complexities of whom Abby was really dating, if anyone.

So Alex walked in silence most of the time. Strangely, though, this suited him pretty well. He had a lot to ponder, so much to process.

And being in the forest, immersed in nature, helped him think things through and even deal with some of the shock and grief from everything that had happened.

Far from the town the air tasted clean and the evil effects of the MeChip felt far away. Except for one stretch of woods a few miles long where the trees were burned and blackened from fire, the life of the forest—the trees, the birdsong, and the occasional snatched sight of squirrel or deer—calmed and soothed him.

It was on the fifth day they saw the tower. They had just passed another part of the forest that had recently burned, the trees rising black and still like sinister sentinels, leafless and lifeless, before passing once more into a place where the foliage grew lush and full. Many leaves had already taken on their fall colors—yellows and reds and every shade of orange—as the days passed and autumn tightened its hold.

They had crested a hill and were about to descend into a small valley when Alex caught sight of something on the far side and higher up a few hundred paces away. Peeking out from above the highest trees was the top of a tower. He pointed it out to the others, who stopped and stared at the concrete construction.

Aside from the trails, a few fire breaks, and the occasional old sign or dilapidated fence, they had seen little evidence of humanity since their run-in with the trigger-happy off-gridders of McCullough's Militia a few days earlier. But this object, gray and hard and utterly out-of-place in the peaceful forest, was clearly something made by people. It was cylindrical, with darker patches near the top that Alex guessed must be windows. Was it a watchtower of some sort? A stronghold? And if so, who or what was it protecting? The others looked as uncertain as Alex felt.

"Should we skirt around it?" Alex's dad asked uncertainly.

"That would take us off the path again, Ben, which I'm reluctant to do if we can help it," Locke answered slowly, shading his eyes with one hand against the autumn sunlight. "Besides, I don't see any sign of life there. But my eyes are old. Perhaps others see something I do not?" he asked, looking around at the younger members of the group. All stared at the edifice up ahead, but each, in turn, shook their heads.

"In that case, I suggest we proceed but keep our eyes and ears open," Locke said.

"And our weapons loaded," Iggy added, shrugging his rifle from off of his back and taking it in both hands.

Slowly they advanced down the hill, every eye trained on the tower.

All appeared normal. There was no sudden movement up ahead, no change in the sounds of the forest, no eerie silence or blast of bullets. The wind rustled lightly among the leaves as it often did, and the occasional chirping of a bird could still be heard. To his right, Alex saw a deer lift its head and look at them as they passed by, then go back to chewing on a bush.

Still, they proceeded cautiously and in silence.

So silently, in fact, that the figure emerging from out of the trees just ten paces ahead of them did not see them. One moment there was no one there. The next, they had stepped out from among the foliage to their right, their back to the group.

"This'll cook up a treat, won't it?" came the voice, high and airy, apparently to no one at all.

She was tall with curly gray hair and dark skin, wearing jeans, knee-high boots, and an ancient leather jacket. In one hand was a fishing rod, in the other a bag, out of which poked the tail of some sort of large fish. For a moment, the group watched in surprise as she started up the hill in the same direction they were heading, still unaware of their presence just a dozen steps behind her.

Then a second creature emerged from the undergrowth.

It was a dog—or more accurately, a hound—huge, its hair as gray as its mistress'. It shambled into view slowly, sniffed the air, turned its head, and saw them. Its eyes fixed on the intruders.

Then it attacked.

16 | Maggie Corbin

The giant beast hurtled towards them, teeth bared, snarling as it prepared to spring upon Locke, who stood at the front of the group.

"Stop!" screamed its owner, her voice loud and commanding.

The creature pulled up just in time.

"Heel, boy. I said heel. Come back here … now!"

Slowly, reluctantly, the wolfhound returned to its mistress' side where it stood facing them making a low, guttural growl.

The immediate danger may have passed but now there was another threat. While their attention had been on the dog, the woman had pulled an old revolver from somewhere inside her jacket. She was pointing it at Locke as she stared at him, brows knitted in suspicion.

"Move and I shoot," she warned.

Iggy looked uncertain. He was still armed, cradling his rifle in both hands, but it was pointing towards the ground. Out of the corner of his eye, Alex could see Iggy studying her carefully as if sizing her up, calculating how quickly she could shoot if he raised his weapon. Locke evidently saw it too, for he stepped in front of Iggy, his palms raised in a sign of peace.

"We mean no harm, I promise you. Iggy, put down your weapon, please," he said quietly.

For a moment Iggy looked as if he might refuse. Then, shrugging, he placed the rifle on the ground in front of him. "Your funeral, old man," he warned in an undertone.

"What do you want? Why are you here?" said the woman. She spoke slowly, all the while looking from one to the other of them suspiciously.

"We're traveling the forest, looking for friends," Locke said calmly, palms still raised.

"Friends? More than ... all of you?" she asked, eyebrows raised.

"Yes. They are two days north of here. In a town among the trees. Have you heard of it? Seen it, perhaps?"

"No, I haven't seen anyone in ... in ... a long time," she said, furrowing her brows as if trying to remember. "A very long time."

"Well, we're looking for them. We think they can help us."

She did not reply but just continued to stare, shaking her head slowly as if she couldn't believe what she was seeing.

"Would you mind if we continued our journey?" Locke asked finally. "This trail is taking us the right way and we were hoping to continue along it. We're just passing through."

"You want to take this ... this path?" she asked, still staring.

"Yes, please."

She looked over her shoulder and up at the tower.

"You can't go in my home."

"Your home?"

"Yes, my home. The big thing there."

"The tower?"

"Yes ... tower ... tower," she replied, repeating the word as if she hadn't heard it in a long time.

"We promise not to go near your home. We really are just passing through," Locke reassured her gently.

"Okay ... fine. But try anything and I shoot. Got it?"

"Understood. And thank you," Locke replied.

The woman stood aside as they passed by in silence. Iggy stooped and slowly picked up his gun by the barrel, showing clearly that he did not intend to use it as he swung it back over his shoulder.

As he walked past, Alex was able to get a better look at her. He guessed she was in her late fifties and was quite striking looking, tall and lean and muscular with high cheekbones and a strong, determined set to her jaw. But the dog was older and frailer than it had first seemed, its eyes cloudy, its muzzle flecked with white hair, its breath wheezy. How had it attacked them with such speed and ferocity, Alex wondered?

Alex was already well up the path when a voice behind him broke the silence.

"Can I pet your dog?"

It was Sybil. She had been at the back of the group. Now she was looking eagerly at the woman, who gaped at her in surprise. Her mouth opened, then shut, then opened again.

"What did you say?"

"Can I pet your dog ... please? It's just I had a dog back home and I miss her and yours looks nice now I see him up close."

The woman stared at Sybil for several seconds, seemingly lost for words.

"Please?" Sybil asked again imploringly, her voice barely more than a whisper.

"Okay, sure ... I guess," said the woman finally, taking a step back and finally lowering her weapon.

Sybil kneeled and held out her hand. The dog sniffed it warily then looked back at its mistress, who shrugged, nodded, and muttered something under her breath.

As if reassured, the dog took a step forward. Sybil let him sniff her, then slowly, gently, stroked his head, finally scratching behind his ears as the dog closed his eyes, evidently enjoying himself.

"Thank you," Sybil said at last as she stood up and rejoined the others, who were standing a little way ahead watching the whole scene. "And I'm Sybil, by the way."

With a last look, they turned and continued up the hill. But they hadn't gone far before the woman called out to them.

"He's called Pete. My dog, I mean. And I'm Maggie ... Maggie Corbin."

"Maggie Corbin?" Locke said in surprise. "But you're from Lincoln." It was a statement, not a question.

"What? Yes. I was from ... from Lincoln. Long time ago now."

"Go ahead," Locke said, turning to the others. "I'll catch you up in a few minutes. Abby, Susanna, can you lead the way?"

With many curious glances, the group trooped up the path and away from Locke, Maggie Corbin, and her dog. As they crested the hill, the last sight Alex had of them was of Locke and Maggie standing on the path, apparently already deep in conversation.

17 | More Mysteries

That night Locke allowed them a new luxury. They had set camp late in the afternoon in a valley ringed by hills on all sides.

"I think we can safely risk a fire here," he announced, immediately cheering everyone up. It had been growing cold at night and the prospect of heat and light could not have been more welcome. What's more, Abby, Harriet, and Sol had formed a hunting party in the hope of finding food.

"How did you catch that?" Tom asked, eyes wide as they returned carrying a full-grown deer.

"Impressive," Alex agreed, shaking his head in wonder.

"Actually, we just got lucky," Harriet admitted as they lay the beast on the ground. "It was lame and so old I think it may have been deaf. It didn't seem to hear us when we crept up on it. Honestly, I don't think it had long to live."

"It was still a great shot," Sol said admiringly.

"Just good fortune," Harriet beamed back.

Luck or not, their success was good news, for food was running short and Alex, for one, was heartily sick of Locke's old stores of stale cookies and dried figs.

As the fire blazed that evening and he sat chewing the freshly-cooked meat, Alex looked around the group and sighed. They'd made it many miles already and Locke seemed confident they were going the right way. Was it possible they might really find the town of Hope after all?

"Can I ask a question, John?" Abby's mom Susanna asked as they sat eating.

"Of course, Susanna."

"I'm curious about the woman we met. Maggie, right? She looked familiar, somehow. What did she say?" As Susanna spoke, Alex noticed Abby sit up, watching Locke with interest.

"Not much that will help us, I fear," Locke said after a pause.

"Really?" Iggy said. "Come on, Locke. She must have said something. You were with her for what—fifteen minutes? Maybe twenty? Don't tell me you were just talking about the weather?"

"Not at all. Well, let me see. She did tell me she had encountered people from a village north of here, although it was a few years ago. I think it may be the town of Hope, although I can't be sure."

"Alright. What else?"

"Well, whoever she encountered was armed, apparently. So we should be on our guard."

"You mean these people might be hostile?" Iggy said.

"I'm not sure. Any place that's trying to avoid government interference is probably going to be cautious about strangers. If they're sensible they'll know how to defend themselves."

"So basically, you don't have any idea if they're going to put on a ticker tape parade for us or just shoot us on sight?" Iggy asked, his voice dripping with sarcasm.

"I doubt either of those things will happen. But we will need to be careful."

"Typical, I don't believe—"

"Will you just drop it, Iggy, huh?" Abby cut in, sounding exasperated. "Can't you see John is doing his best? We're all doing our best. Can't we all just get along?"

"Oh so it's 'John' now is it? Hey, all I'm doing is asking questions, alright? Is there anything wrong—"

But Abby gave Iggy such a furious look he seemed to think better of what he was about to say.

"Fine, fine!" he said, holding up his hands in mock surrender. Picking up his food again, he fell silent.

"Did you know that woman, John?" Susanna asked after a pause.

"Yes, I did," Locke answered. "Maggie and I knew each other in Lincoln. But it was a long time ago."

"And?" asked Tom curiously.

"It's an old story and not really ... um ... relevant to our situation now," Locke answered as he stared thoughtfully into the fire.

"How long has she been in the woods?" Abby asked at last.

"Several years. She seems somehow to have become liberated from the MeChip's control—she didn't seem to know exactly how—and fled to the forest. She's been here alone—just her and her dog Pete—ever since."

"Why didn't you invite her to come with us? Then she wouldn't be alone anymore," Sybil asked.

"I did. But I don't think she's ready to be around other people. Even our small group must have seemed overwhelming after so much time alone. Now, who wants to help me make some hot chocolate?"

"Dr. Locke, can I ask you something?" asked Harriet a few minutes later, her fingers cupped around a stainless-steel mug of steaming hot chocolate.

"Of course."

"It's probably a stupid question, really, but I was wondering ... why does hardly anyone have siblings?"

Locke took a long time to answer. Finally, he set down his hot chocolate and started to speak, staring once more into the fire as the logs crackled and burned.

"There are at least two reasons, Harriet. One is the MeChip has been programmed to discourage couples from wanting too many children."

"Why?"

"I'm not sure, exactly. That decision came after my time. But I suspect it comes down to money: how many workers the corporate elites need in the future and how many mouths they want to feed."

"Alright," Harriet said slowly. "What else? You said there were two reasons."

"Well, the other reason ... a much worse reason, is that many children die."

"What?" said several people at once.

"The corporate elites who run our country have cut investment in our hospitals, allowed dangerous chemicals to run into our rivers and water supplies, and let air pollution go unchecked. This means people don't live as long as they should. Children die of diseases we had previously wiped out, and parents perish before their time."

"That's horrible," Sybil said, aghast.

"I agree. But I'm sorry to say the people who run our country don't care about their fellow citizens, only about power and money. They consider most of us to be expendable."

There was silence as people digested this awful news.

"Do they replace them? The kids, I mean?" Harriet asked eventually in a quiet voice.

"Occasionally. But they won't unless they have a very strong reason to do so," Locke replied, looking at Alex, who found himself thinking back to that night when the Fixers had come to replace him. "It's easier for them to program people's MeChips so they forget their siblings than to replace them."

"What about adults? Do they always replace them?" Abby asked, clearly thinking of her father, her fingers clenching into fists as she spoke.

"Again, it depends on the circumstances. But imagine, for instance, that one family has been devastated by a disease and only a single parent remains. Sometimes it would make sense to combine that person with a family where just one parent has recently passed away."

"But why? Why not just let them live their lives as a single person or a smaller family? Why not allow people to know the truth that someone they love has died?"

"That interferes with the story—the myth—the MeChip peddles that life is good. If people die before their time, if families are broken into pieces with the loss of a parent or a child, then folks will start to question whether life is that good after all. On top of that, at least some of the elites believe in the traditional family, where a child has a mother and a father. So wherever possible they will keep that group intact, even if it means replacing dead parents from time to time and using the MeChip programming to suppress people's memories."

"It's disgusting!" said Abby angrily as her mom put an arm around her daughter's shoulders.

There was another lengthy silence. Finally, Harriet got up and walked to the edge of the clearing, biting her lip. Alex thought he saw tears in her eyes. Had she, too, remembered something from her past?

"What's with her?" Tom whispered to Alex and Sol, who were sitting near him. Alex could only shrug, mystified, but a moment later Sol stood up and followed her.

"Do the ... the replacements know? I mean, do they know they're not really the kid's mom or dad?" Abby asked Locke after another pause, her voice sounding shaky and tense.

"No," Locke said sadly. "They're as much victims of this as anyone else. In the case of the man who replaced your father, for instance, it is quite likely his wife had died, just as your father did, and the MeChip hid the memory of that trauma from him."

"Then what—" Alex's dad began, but Locke held up a hand.

"I'm sorry, Ben, but I think that's more than enough for everyone to process for one night. We can talk more tomorrow if you like, but for now, we should all try to get some sleep."

Iggy opened his mouth to speak—perhaps to object—but stopped when his mom put a restraining hand on his arm and shook her head. Alex felt relieved. He was thoroughly sick of Iggy's sniping.

As he lay in his dark tent half an hour later, Alex could hear several people's regular, deep breathing. But sleep would not come to him. When he closed his eyes, the image of Abby's fake father kept intruding, followed by Abby's expression of anger and disgust by the fireside at what the elites had done to her family. Confused questions kept crowding in: why was Iggy so aggressive towards Locke? Why had Locke ended the conversation when he did? Was there something he didn't want to talk about ... something he was hiding? Just who was the mysterious Maggie Corbin and how well did Locke really know her? And who would remember something next? As Alex finally drifted into an uneasy sleep, his last clear thought was that the truth to these questions, when it finally emerged, may make him feel worse than simply not knowing.

18 | The Guitarist's Secret

The next day began badly. It started raining as they set out, turning into a heavy downpour that soaked into clothes and skin, seeming to reach their bones. Alex shivered, hoping his X-guitar, which he'd carried all the way from Lincoln, would stay dry under its makeshift plastic wrapping. Not for the first time he wondered why he was bringing it with him. What possible use could a guitar have here in the forest? Still, he felt strangely reluctant to abandon this link to Lincoln and his past life. Besides, he'd carried it this far. There was no point giving up now, especially if Locke was right and the town of Hope was not too far away.

They had covered only a few miles as they trudged along, the trail still leading them gradually higher into the hills and closer to the mountains. No one was speaking and Alex was simply concentrating on putting one foot in front of another when the person in front of him stopped and he bumped into them. It was Locke. Abby and Susanna, standing on either side of the old man, had halted too, staring ahead of them and rooted to the spot. As the others caught up, Locke raised his hand and motioned them to silence. Alex craned to look over Locke's shoulder—and drew a breath.

The creature was large, much bigger than the heaviest human; a vast mass blocking the path just 30 yards ahead. Its coat of short black fur was dripping with water as it stood, its head raised, sniffing the air. It turned in their direction, its small black eyes fixed on them. Humans and bear eyed each other warily for several long seconds. Iggy and Harriet cautiously raised their rifles and trained them on the animal, Abby notched an arrow and slowly raised her bow, while Locke pulled out a can of bear-repellent spray and told them in a fierce whisper not to fire unless he gave the word.

The beast took a step towards them and stopped, apparently unsure what to do as it surveyed the group. Alex felt like it was looking at each of them in turn, sizing them up. Over the mountains lightning flashed, followed seconds later by the rumble of distant thunder. The bear turned its head towards the north, as if searching for the source of the light. It looked back in their direction, still studying them.

Finally, slowly, it turned away and lumbered off the path into the undergrowth. Alex exhaled slowly, realizing only now he'd been holding his breath all this time.

"What now?" Tom asked finally.

"Now we wait," Locke answered.

They stood in silence, listening and straining their eyes and ears for any sign of the animal as the rain continued to fall in sheets. But the massive creature didn't return. Eventually, they proceeded past the place it had crossed before hurrying on their way.

By mid-afternoon the storm had passed, its dark clouds scudding off to the east. The sun was now blazing, almost making Alex feel like it was summer again. His clothes gradually dried and the group made excellent progress, covering many miles before Locke called a halt early in the evening.

Once more, they camped that night in a valley where Locke felt it would be safe to light a fire, and the hunting party came back from a nearby stream with several fish, which Alex's father Ben said were trout.

After cooking and deboning the fish, the group sat around the fire and ate their food. In spite of the change in weather and delicious meal, however, most of them were silent and withdrawn. Tom was shooting angry glances at Iggy, who was sitting next to Sybil. Harriet still seemed subdued and lost in thought, while Abby was avoiding looking at either Alex or Iggy.

Only John Locke seemed in good spirits.

"If my calculations are correct we should reach the town of Hope by tomorrow afternoon," he announced, smiling at them all. "Surely that's worth celebrating?"

No one seemed enthusiastic. A minute later, he tried again.

"How about some music? Alex, you've carried that guitar all the way from Lincoln. Why don't you play something to cheer us up?"

"But it's ... it's electric and we don't have an amp," Alex replied awkwardly, feeling vaguely irritated at being put on the spot like this.

"Oh, I'm sure it'll be fine. Go on, give it a try," Locke said encouragingly.

"Alright," Alex replied grudgingly as he unwrapped the instrument. To his relief, the guitar didn't need much tuning, so he sat with it on his lap and started to play.

He tried out an old Retro-Romwave number first. It was simple and downbeat, a bit melancholy in fact, which suited his mood. When he finished, Locke and a few others clapped.

"That was wonderful. Now how about something more cheerful?" Locke said.

Alex played a famous Rock Shop number. Of course, it didn't sound the same without an amplifier, not to mention the bass and drums. But it was catchy and fun and by the end of the song, most of the others had joined in and were singing the chorus. He did a few more pieces along the same lines and each time the others sang along. Smiles started to replace the earlier somber looks as the group started enjoying themselves.

Locke had been right, Alex realized as he finished up another song. Music had lifted their mood.

"Go on, Alex, do another," Tom urged as Alex finally placed the guitar on the ground next to him.

"That's all from me, Tom. Always leave them wanting more, remember?" Alex replied, winking at his friend.

"Does anyone else want to play?" Locke asked. "Iggy, how about you?"

To Alex's surprise, Iggy shook his head. "No amp, no performance," he said flatly as his mother Alice glared at him and Tom rolled his eyes.

"Don't you play, Ben?" Alice asked, looking at Alex's dad.

"That's right!" Susanna said suddenly. "I remember now; you performed years ago at a school fundraiser," she said, smiling at the memory. "You were good, too. Go on, play something."

Locke opened his mouth to speak but evidently thought better of it. Meanwhile, Tom had picked up the guitar and handed it to Alex's dad. He looked reluctant to take it, but after a moment's hesitation accepted the object, taking it in both hands. He stared at it for a few seconds before slowly, awkwardly placing it on his lap.

"It's been a while. I kinda decided to stop playing a few years ago, you know," he said uncertainly, looking up at the group.

"Now I remember that, too," Susanna said. "But I never understood why, Ben. You were so good."

"You know, I'd rather not," he said.

"Go on, Ben. You can do it. Play something, anything. Please!" Susanna said, smiling encouragingly.

There was a long silence as Ben stared at the guitar. He tried a chord but it came out all wrong, the sound discordant and jarring. He tried once more. Again, it sounded all wrong. Dissonant and harsh, it wasn't even close to any chord Alex recognized. Apparently defeated, Ben pushed the guitar away from him and onto the dirt, muttering to himself.

"Dad, what's up?" Alex asked, his heart beating strangely fast. "You can't have forgotten how to play. Start with the easy stuff. How about something that opens in E minor?"

His father's face had turned red but his mother's, Alex saw, was deathly pale.

"I haven't forgotten," Ben said quietly.

"Then why don't you play something?" Alex asked, noticing as he spoke that his hands were trembling.

"I can't. I haven't forgotten because I ... I never knew how to play."

"Yes you did, Ben," Susanna insisted, looking confused. "You played all the time."

"No, I didn't, Susanna. I've never played guitar before in my life."

"But Dad, that's not true. Tell me it isn't true," Alex begged, his voice cracking as he began to understand.

"I'm sorry, son. But I can't lie to you. I'm not the man who used to—"

"No!" Alex's mom interrupted, her voice shaking. "You can't tell them. Not now, not yet," she begged, putting a restraining hand on her husband's arm. Gently, he took her hand in his own, looking into her eyes and shaking his head.

"I have to tell them the truth," he replied firmly.

"The truth about what, Dad?" Alex asked as a sense of fear, of panic, rose inside him. No one spoke—no one seemed to be even breathing—as they all stared at Alex's father. But he could not meet their eyes, looking into the flames of the fire as he replied.

"I never played guitar before, Alex, because I'm not Ben Franklin ... because I'm not your real father."

19 | The Replacement

Alex sprang to his feet—he had no idea why—and stood staring down at the man seated on the ground. His brain felt like it would explode, his heart was galloping out of control as adrenaline coursed through him.

"You *are* my dad!" Alex declared angrily, daring this man to contradict him.

"I wish I was. I wish it with all my heart. But I'm not. I'm a replacement," he replied flatly, still unable to meet Alex's gaze.

"Stop pranking me, Dad. This isn't funny. It's not funny!" he yelled.

Alex was breathing in ragged, uneven gasps as if he'd just run a marathon. He balled his hands into fists and leaned forward on his toes as if ready to launch himself at someone, to fight, to attack.

The man Alex had believed was his father stood up and finally returned Alex's gaze. He looked weary, his shoulders slumped, his forehead corrugated with lines Alex had never seen before. The glint of a tear leaked from the corner of one eye.

"I'm sorry," the man said simply.

Alex wanted to do something, do *anything*. For a millisec he felt an urge to leap at this man and pummel him until he admitted he was lying, pranking him, pranking all of them. But as he looked into his eyes—those eyes he knew so well—the fight went out of him. Alex knew this person was telling the truth. It was not because some clear memory stolen by the MeChip had just returned fully formed. He could recall nothing remotely helpful right now, although a dimly-remembered recurring nightmare had hinted at the truth. But somehow he knew—just knew, deep down—that this man was not his father.

Alex exhaled slowly, feeling the adrenaline drain from him. He was weary and defeated, like a boxer knocked to the canvas and knowing numbly he won't be able to get back to his feet before the count of ten. He was dimly aware of everyone watching him. Abby was biting her lip while Tom was looking horrified, his mouth open and gaping.

"Why didn't you tell me?" Alex asked eventually, looking back at the man.

"I only remembered a few days ago," he replied simply.

"We were planning to tell you when we got to Hope, Alex. It was just a lot to take in. We're still dealing with it ourselves," his mother chimed in, her face still deathly pale.

"And what about my dad: my real father?" Alex asked

"He's ... gone," his mom said. "I don't remember clearly but it was about five years ago. He got sick one day and just ... just died," she said, putting a hand to her mouth as she tried to hold back tears.

"So they brought you in to replace him?" Alex asked, turning back to face the man.

"Yes. I remembered a few days ago; just woke up with a memory of arriving at your house late one night. I guess that's when the MeChip made me believe I played the guitar but had decided to quit. Because your real father played, but I never did. It was probably easier for the MeChip to make me think I used to play and had stopped than to make you all forget your dad was a guitarist."

"And did you know you were a replacement?" Alex asked, staring in disbelief at this imposter, this fake father.

"Of course not! I wouldn't have done it if I'd known. I'm not a monster. At least I ... I don't think I am," he said, wiping a hand across his face. "The truth is, Alex, I don't know *who* I am. I have a dim memory now of someone else—a wife, I guess. But she's dead, too. I don't remember the details, but I know she's gone. I don't remember her name. I don't even remember my own," he said, finally breaking down and covering his face with both hands as Alex's mom put an arm across his shoulder, tears now streaming from her eyes.

As Alex witnessed their grief a surge of pity welled up inside him for this man, this stranger. And then there was his mom; what must she be going through? He wanted to reach out, to try to comfort them, but felt rooted to the spot, drained and confused and numb and angry all at once.

"So what happens now?" he asked at last.

"I don't know exactly," his mom answered, wiping her eyes. "But I do know this. He may not be the man I married, but we have been together five years now. And he's a good man," she said, taking his hand.

"Liz is right," the man said. "Five years *is* a long time. The MeChip lied to us about a lot of things, but we know for sure there are real feelings here. So we're going to give it a go. Support each other. See what happens."

There was another lengthy silence as Alex took all of this in.

"And I'm ... I'm here for you, too," the man added after a pause, looking earnestly at Alex.

"Here for what? You're not my father! You just admitted it. My real father's gone. Dead," Alex snarled, his anger rising again.

"Alex, please," his mom implored, reaching out and putting a hand on his shoulder. But Alex shrugged it away.

"Don't blame them, Alex. They're just as much victims as you are," John Locke said, breaking his silence and rising slowly to his feet.

Alex turned to face him as a suspicion formed in his mind.

"You knew, didn't you? You knew all about this."

Locke didn't answer but for a millisec his eyes flickered away, unable to hold Alex's gaze.

"I knew it! How long have you known about this and not told anyone? A week? A year? More?" Alex yelled.

"I've known about it since it happened," Locke admitted with a sigh.

"Then why didn't you do something?" Alex said, barely able to believe his ears.

"I did do something, Alex. I made my plans to defeat the MeChip. It took years of thinking, researching, planning, preparing. Finally, when I was ready, I contacted you. It's all connected," Locke said, trying to explain.

"How?" Iggy asked, jumping to his feet and sounding as angry as Alex. "How is it connected, exactly? How is Alex's dad dying connected to your so-called plan to beat the MeChip? How does that even make sense? Why don't you explain it to us, huh?"

"I ... I can't. Not everything, not yet," Locke replied.

"Why not? Why can't you tell us the truth?" Alex shouted.

"Yeah," Iggy agreed. "You're always talking about honesty and how the MeChip's made all these lies, but you're just as bad. You won't tell us what's really going on," he said, glaring at Locke.

Alex was so angry now he took a step towards Locke, then another. A moment later, though, Tom and Sol were on their feet and alongside him, each holding an arm.

"You've got to calm down, Alex. Seriously," Sol said, looking worried.

"I *am* calm," Alex insisted, knowing it wasn't true. Looking down, he saw that he had unconsciously balled his hands into fists again as he glared at Locke, as if ready to fight.

"Alright then, I'm not calm," he admitted, unclenching his fists and pointing a finger accusingly at Locke. "And I'm not going to calm down until that man starts telling us the truth!"

"Alex is right. Enough is enough. You're hiding stuff from us, old man. Time to tell us everything," Iggy insisted, siding with his rival.

"I will tell you everything, I promise you. But only when the time is right," Locke replied.

"And until then we just have to keep discovering these secrets—these landmines—all by ourselves?" Alex spat as Iggy nodded. "You have the nerve to ask us to tell you when we remember things when all this time you know everything anyway!"

"It's not like that," Locke said defensively. "I don't know everything. Not by a long stretch. And I don't want to ... to overload you. Some of what I know would be too much right now. It wouldn't help anyone."

"Who says? Why should you get to decide what we should and shouldn't know, huh?" Iggy asked.

"I shouldn't, Iggy," Locke conceded "No one should have that right. And I could be wrong, I admit it. But I have to use my best judgment on what to say and when to say it. For now, I've told you everything I think you should know."

"That's not—"

"Let me finish, please! I will tell you more in the coming days ... more when we reach Hope. But I cannot—I will not—say more for now. I beg you to trust me on this."

"Well, I don't," Alex said, folding his arms and glaring at this man he'd thought he could believe in.

"Me neither!" Iggy chimed in, striding forward to stand by his new ally.

20 | Alex and Abby

Alex yawned. Again. He had slept badly, unable to find peace as an endless flurry of thoughts assailed him, buzzing around in his head like angry bees. When he had finally dozed off, his slumber had been fitful at best. Eventually, he had just given up, slipping silently out of the tent just as the first rays of morning light peaked over the hills to the east.

As he stood there shivering slightly from the cold, from the corner of his vision came a flash of red light illuminating the sky to the south. He spun around and rubbed his eyes, unsure if what he'd seen was real or if his weary mind was playing tricks with him. He scanned the horizon, waiting for it to happen again. It didn't.

He wondered if he should wake Locke and tell him, then decided against it. The last thing he wanted to do right now was talk to that man. The light had probably just been his imagination anyway, he decided. Eventually, he found a nearby log and sat down as anger, confusion, and sheer exhaustion struggled for ascendancy.

By midday, his mood had, if anything, gotten worse. They had walked several hours, still going uphill most of the time. Rain was falling, light but persistent. The temperature had dropped, too. It may only be October, but winter came early up here. He had rebuffed several attempts by his mother, Tom, Sol, Locke, and even his fake father to engage him in conversation. Why wouldn't they leave him alone, give him a chance to think? Only Iggy of all people seemed to have understood: he had nodded a brief greeting to Alex over breakfast, nothing more. No attempt to make him talk, just a nod and a millisec's eye contact that seemed to say it all. *I get it. I know what it feels like to not have a father. I'm on your side.*

They stopped for a brief rest and a bite to eat early in the afternoon. Locke dished out more of his old stock of stale cookies—just two each now as supplies ran low. Alex took them without speaking and walked away from the group, eager to be alone.

"Don't go far, Alex!" Locke called after him. "Remember, we're probably getting near to Hope. We should stay close."

Alex ignored him and stomped off the path, wending his way between the trees. But he didn't go far. Grudgingly, he knew Locke was right. They should stick together. He soon found himself in a small glade. It was too wet to sit on the ground but there was a large rock on the far side. He sat down and looked in the direction of the path. Voices carried softly and he could just make out Sol and Harriet through a gap in the trees, although the others were hidden from view.

The cookie was hard and bland. For a millisec, he was tempted to throw it away, but then he thought better of it. If Locke couldn't find Hope soon and with this weather making hunting harder, he'd be grateful for every scrap of sustenance he could get, no matter how flavorless.

His mind was just turning once more to last night's revelation, replaying the scene in his head for the twentieth time or more, when he realized he was no longer alone.

Abby entered the clearing, caught sight of him, and stopped. She looked at him, head tilted to one side.

"Can I sit here?" she asked, nodding at the rock.

"Sure. It's big enough for two," he shrugged, shifting a little to make room.

Setting her bow and quiver of arrows on the ground, she sat down but didn't speak. As the silence lengthened Alex found himself feeling two diametrically opposed emotions: a strong desire for her to stay here with him and an equally powerful urge to run away from her, to be alone.

"Can I ask you a question?" she said finally, turning to face him.

"Sure, since you already did," he replied, looking at her and trying, but failing, to crack a smile.

"Are you okay, Alex?" she asked. "I mean, I know you're not since … well, since I kinda know what you're going through, but …" she trailed off as if unsure what to say next.

"I'm not okay," Alex admitted, trying to keep his emotions in check. "It's just … a lot, you know. But how about you, Abby? I mean, I'm not the only one who's lost his dad."

Abby sighed. "How are we supposed to deal with something like this? I feel so confused and mad and sad all at the same time. And then there's my mom. She really needs me and I'm not sure what to do or say to make things right. But I'll deal with it. I mean, what choice do I have?"

Alex turned to look at her properly for the first time. Up close she appeared exhausted, with dark circles under red-rimmed eyes. She was still *uber* tidy, though, Alex had to admit as she held his gaze.

"Why wouldn't you talk to me all week?" he said finally, surprising himself with the question. "I mean, I know you've been going through hell but I just wanted to help, to be there for you. And instead, you're spending most of the time with Locke and—"

"I know and I'm sorry," Abby cut in. "I wanted to talk to you but I've been really confused. At first, I just wanted to be alone with my thoughts, then I wanted to talk with my mom and—"

"I get that you needed time at first, but why push me away? I mean, you've been off-gridding me the whole time."

"I know. It's hard to explain. When I found out you knew about my dad being taken away … well, I needed to work through that."

"I get it. But you don't blame me, do you? I mean, I tried to tell—"

"Of course I don't blame you, Alex. I realize now you did your best. But it's not that that's kept me away."

"Then what?" Alex asked, curious. It took her several seconds before she finally answered him.

"The truth is, I've started having these memories about Iggy and about ... well, about you and me. It's really thrown me for a loop."

"What kind of memories?"

"I thought I'd been dating Iggy for the past few months. But now I'm remembering something different. It's still *uber* fuzzy, but now my MeChip's off I feel like there's something else that happened. Something to do with you and me," she said, looking away as her cheeks and neck turned red.

She was about to say more when someone else entered the clearing.

The intruder stopped, eyes flicking from one to the other of them.

"What are you two doing here?" he said, his voice arrogant and accusing.

It was Iggy.

21 | Triangle in a Circle

"I asked what you're doing here?" he repeated, eyes narrowed as he advanced into the small circle of the clearing.

"Just talking," Alex replied. "Nothing wrong with that, is there?"

"It depends," Iggy replied.

"On what?"

"On whether you can tell me why my girlfriend is off-gridding me and talking to a dexter like you instead?"

Alex sighed. His new alliance with Iggy hadn't even lasted a day. He was about to reply when Abby spoke.

"I'm not ignoring you, Iggy. I just needed some space to figure things out."

"What's there to figure out?" Iggy asked angrily.

"What's really happening with us."

"You know what's happening, Abby. We're dating. We've been together, what, six months at least."

"Have we?"

"You know we have."

"I'm not so sure. That's why I was talking with Alex just now. I have a feeling he might know something, remember something."

"What can this dexter remember about us?" Iggy asked, raising an eyebrow. "This is none of his business. Why do you care what he might say about us dating?"

"You're not," Alex said quietly.

"What?" Abby and Iggy said at once.

"You're not dating. It was a false memory implanted by the MeChip."

"What are you talking about, Franklin?" Iggy asked, his voice getting louder.

"You're not dating Abby. You never were."

"Have you gone smeckin' crazy?"

"No, Iggy. I'm not sure why, but the MeChip deceived you. You were going out with Charlotte Riedesel until a few weeks ago. Don't you remember?"

"Charlotte Riedesel? No way!"

"Yes way, Iggy. You just broke up with her at the start of term. You were dating the whole summer. Everyone knew about it."

"But that's not ... then how could Abby and I ..." Iggy said, his voice trailing off as he paused, a look of intense concentration on his face as he scratched his now-stubbly chin.

"That's what I'm trying to tell you guys," Alex insisted. "I have no idea why, but the MeChip implanted a memory that you two were dating, when in fact Abby and I were—"

"Wait, what?" Iggy interrupted. "First you're telling me Abby and I aren't an item and now you're trying to claim you two were?"

"Not exactly—"

"Not exactly? Not ever, Franklin. I mean, why would she go out with a dexter like you when she could have me, huh?" Iggy said scornfully. He took a step towards Alex, who stood up. As they faced each other, Alex was dimly aware of other voices nearby. But he was too intent on his rival to pay attention to them. Whatever was going on with Locke and the others, it couldn't be more important than this.

"Hey, do I get a say in any of this?" Abby asked, getting to her feet and stepping between them. "I'm not some prize you can win, you know. It's my decision who I date!" she insisted, glaring from one of them to the other.

"Not until I teach this smeckin' dexter a lesson," Iggy said, sidestepping her and pushing a finger into Alex's chest. "I don't know why you think pranking us like this is funny, Franklin, but I won't put up with it."

"I'm not pranking anyone," Alex insisted, his voice louder, too, as he raised his fists and squared off against his rival, waiting for the attack he felt sure was coming.

Iggy drew back his arm, fist clenched, ready to throw the first punch.

It never landed. At that moment, a shot rang out, then a blaster flashed between the trees, Iggy whirled round and reached for his rifle, which was still strapped to his back, while Abby plucked her bow and quiver of arrows from the ground and Alex peered among the trees.

"No. No! Stop!" screamed a voice he recognized.

It was Alex's mom.

22 | Firefight in the Forest

A second laser beam flashed and Alex heard a loud grunt, followed by a scream. He began running, tearing through the trees, ignoring the branches tugging at his arms, the thorns tearing at his skin, and the roots trying to trip him. Abby shouted something but he couldn't make out the words. They didn't matter. Getting to his mom was the only thing that mattered.

He burst through the trees and onto the path, smashing into the back of someone he didn't recognize. She was wearing olive-green fatigues and a sage-colored jacket. The girl—who looked about his own age—went sprawling to the ground, dropping a laser pistol. Without thinking Alex lunged for it, grabbing the weapon with his right hand while pushing her back down to the ground with his left as she tried to stand. She fell back as he cast a quick glance up the trail.

The scene was chaotic. Three green-clad warriors stood a few yards away, their guns pointed at Locke, Sybil, Tom, Susanna, and Alice, whose hands were raised. Meanwhile, another unknown soldier was firing his laz-rifle off the path towards the far trees, where Alex caught a fleeting glimpse of a figure speeding away, rifle in hand. Was that Harriet?

He heard a noise behind him and spun around. His heart jolted. His fake father—the imposter—was kneeling, tending to a fallen figure lying prone on the ground, her face ashen, her eyes closed.

It was his mom. The front of her jacket was charred and blackened and a thin tendril of smoke was curling slowly from her chest. Close by stood another soldier, his back to Alex, his weapon trained on Alex's mom.

"What the smeck have you done to her?" the man Alex had believed was his father shouted at this unknown combatant, his voice shaking with emotion.

Without pausing to think, Alex ran forward and brought the butt of the laser blaster slamming down on the enemy soldier's head. The man grunted and slumped to the ground as Alex pushed him aside and knelt by his mom. He put his ear to her mouth, straining to hear something, anything.

For a moment, nothing. Then ... a gentle exhalation.

"She's alive, Dad, she's alive!" he said without thinking. "Get her off the path. Hide. I'll deal with them," he instructed, instantly turning to face the enemy.

"Put the gun down, child!"

The order came from an older woman with graying, shoulder-length hair and cold, gray eyes. Like the others, she was clad in green. She held a combat laz-rifle—an old model, but deadly enough. It was pointing directly at Alex. Two of her comrades had turned around to face him too, while another still covered Locke and the group that had already surrendered and who were now seated on the ground. Another enemy was still blazing away at something hidden among the trees.

"No!" said the girl Alex had disarmed. She stood up, blocking her comrade's aim and speaking directly to the older woman. "Don't shoot him, Captain Bailey, please!"

For a moment no one moved. Captain Bailey seemed stunned by her younger comrade's intervention.

"If you put down your gun, no one will be hurt, I promise," said the girl, turning towards Alex, her green eyes fixed on his, her voice pleading.

Alex hesitated, looking around at where his mom had been. Already she was gone from sight, carried into the trees by Alex's phony father while the green-eyed girl had been speaking. Alex caught Locke's eye and the old man nodded, as if signaling for him to listen to her entreaty.

But before he could reply the crack of a rifle sounded from out of the woods to his right, the bullet splintering a tree trunk near the enemy troops. A second shot rang out. One of the green-clad warriors screamed and dropped his laz-rifle, clutching his shoulder and falling backwards.

It was now or never. Alex dived among the bushes, narrowly dodging a barrage of laser blasts. He scampered through the trees, keeping his head down as he ran towards the sound of the rifles.

A millisec later and he saw them. Harriet and Iggy were both armed, keeping up a steady fire with their rifles from concealed positions behind two trees. Abby pulled the string back on her bow and let loose an arrow, while Sol squatted nearby trying to stay out of the line of fire while looking for makeshift weapons. As Alex looked on, Sol found a broken branch that might serve as a club.

"Don't hit the others! They've been captured and are back on the path," Alex urged Iggy, Harriet, and Abby as he joined them.

"We're not idiots, Franklin," Iggy shouted back over the noise of the blasters. "You stay here and keep them pinned down," he instructed, noticing Alex's gun. "I'm going to skirt around the edge, catch them from behind. Abby, are you coming?"

Without waiting for an answer, Iggy darted away to the right, rifle at the ready. A moment later, Abby had followed him, ducking low to avoid being seen, bow in hand.

Alex aimed his laser pistol and fired, aiming high to make sure none of his friends were hit. Harriet looked over at him and nodded in approval. Then her eyes widened.

"Alex, behind you!" she screamed.

Alex whirled around, lifted his gun ... too late!

Something heavy smashed into the side of his head. He fell to his knees, dazed, then toppled backwards, landing among the dead leaves that littered the forest floor. His last sight as he sank into unconsciousness was of the girl he'd disarmed standing above him, all talk of peace evidently forgotten as she stood, another blaster now in hand, her green eyes blazing as she aimed at someone he couldn't see.

23 | Ticks and Tweezers

Someone was wiping his forehead. He could feel the soft, cool touch of a moistened towel being gently dabbed across his skin. He opened his eyes, discerned a face above him coming in and out of focus. She had green eyes and light, copper-colored hair that curled into ringlets at the ends.

For a moment he had no idea who she was. Then the memory came rushing back. The girl in green. The attack! He tried to sit up but could not move. Something was holding him down.

"What happened? Where am I?" he asked, his voice hoarse as if he hadn't used it in a long time.

"Safe enough. For now," she replied, surveying him calmly.

"But where am I?"

"Hope."

"Then we made it," he sighed. "But why did you attack us? And where's my mom?"

"We didn't attack you. You attacked us. At least, your friends did," she replied calmly. "And your mom's fine. She was checked by Doctor Blackwell and released earlier today. She's with the others now being judged."

"Being judged? For what?" Alex asked, struggling once more to move but again finding it impossible.

"For attacking our patrol."

"But we wouldn't have ... Locke wouldn't have—"

"That's for the mayor to decide. Lie still, please. I need to check your head and clean your wound."

Ignoring his other questions, she firmly moved his head to one side with her hand.

"Hmm, still swollen. I'm going to apply some antiseptic to the wound. This will sting."

It did. He gasped as she applied the ointment.

"There, all done, I think, but ... oh, no."

"What?"

"You have a tick. Behind your ear."

"A what?"

"A tick. You know, little critters that live in forests? Carry Lyme disease? No? Well, I'll need to remove it. Wait here a minute."

"Like I have any choice," he muttered. He tried to sit up but still found it impossible. Casting his eyes down, he saw some sort of rope or belt strapped across his chest and arms.

"Hey, why am I tied up?" he asked.

"Captain Bailey's orders until the mayor decides what to do with you," she said over her shoulder as she busied herself at a cabinet. Alex briefly scanned the room and saw three other beds—two empty, the other with a curtain pulled around it. There was a single wooden door on the far wall, a desk with an old computer and antique printer, a few medical instruments, and several shelves and cabinets. Everything in the place looked old—even ancient—although all was clean and scrubbed, from the lustrous white walls to the gleaming metal shelves and polished tiled floor.

After opening a couple of drawers, his captor came back holding a small, stainless-steel device. It was the size of a pair of tweezers, like a miniature metal pencil ending in two sharp points.

"What are you planning on doing with that?" Alex asked, eyeing it nervously.

"I'm going to remove the tick. Don't worry, it won't hurt. Much."

Alex wasn't sure, but he thought he caught the flicker of a smile playing across the corner of her lips.

"Are you even allowed to do this? You look way too young to be a doctor or a nurse."

"I'm fifteen. And no, I'm not trained. Or qualified. I just snuck in here since I like doing this stuff for fun. Now, hold still while I take this thing out."

He tried to pull away, turning his head to the side. She looked at him, eyebrows raised, definitely smiling now.

"Seriously? Look, I'm a trainee medic, okay? Doctor Blackwell's teaching me. I'm going to be a doctor myself one day. And this is seriously the easiest thing to do. I've been removing ticks since I was a little kid. You really don't need to worry. Now hold still."

Reluctantly he lay there, resisting the urge to wrench his head away as he felt the metal touch the skin behind his left ear. The young medic narrowed her eyes as she looked at the side of his head, ran the device along the side of his skin, and gently but firmly pulled away.

"And here it is," she said, holding the creature up for Alex to see. A small bug was trapped between the two metal points, half-a-dozen legs wriggling randomly as it attempted to escape.

"Ew, gross!" Alex said as the girl looked at it dispassionately.

She walked back over to the cabinet and dropped the tick into a small glass containing what looked to Alex like water.

"What did you just do to it?" he asked.

"I put it in rubbing alcohol. It kills them."

"Why not just step on it?"

"Not safe. It may be infectious."

"With line disease?" Alex asked, starting to feel nervous again.

"Not line disease, Lyme disease. L-Y-M-E. Jeez, what the smeck do they teach you chipslaves anyway?"

"What?"

"Nothing. But yeah, infected with Lyme disease. That's something you don't want to get, believe me."

"Could I have it already?" Alex asked, licking his lips nervously.

"Maybe, but probably not. Usually it's the nymphs—the young ticks—that carry it. Yours was definitely an adult. Plus, it typically has to be attached for a couple of days. This looks like it had barely fed on you at all—it probably climbed aboard when you were knocked out in the forest yesterday. Now, hold still again while I clean the bite area with antiseptic."

Again she approached and he tried to stay still. As she leaned over him dabbing behind his ear, Alex found himself feeling disoriented, relieved, anxious, and embarrassed all at the same time. He risked a glance at her face, trying to read her personality or mood in those green eyes, but her attention was focused solely on the task at hand.

She was still dabbing gently behind his ear when the door crashed open. Abby rushed in, followed by Tom and Sol.

"Alex, it's okay. We're free. The mayor believes us!" she said as she dashed towards him, still grinning.

It was only then she became fully aware of the other girl, her hand still touching Alex's face.

"And who the smeck is this?" Abby asked, her voice suddenly hard and cold.

24 | Leah

"I ... I don't know her name," Alex said uncertainly.

"But you're letting her stroke your face?" Abby asked accusingly as she tilted her head to one side and narrowed her eyes, her lip curling in disbelief. Behind Abby, Tom was gazing at the scene open-mouthed, while Sol was biting his lip.

"I'm not stroking his face!" the young medic replied furiously, standing up and facing Abby, hands on hips and green eyes blazing, her anger matching Abby's own. "I'm cleaning his wound."

"You're what?" Abby said, now on the back foot.

"Cleaning his wound. And removing a tick, too."

"A what?" Abby repeated, looking even more confused.

"A bug. I'm a medic. Well, a trainee medic. My name's Leah Mecon," she added stonily.

"Oh," Abby said more quietly. "Then sorry, I guess," she added, her face reddening as her voice fell away to a whisper.

"So you can relax, whoever you are. Your boyfriend's perfectly safe and recovering well. Now I need to speak with Doctor Blackwell. Excuse me."

"He's not my ..." Abby began, trailing off as Leah Mecon strode past them to the door and left the room without another word.

For a few seconds, no one spoke. Then the door opened again and Alex's mom burst in, followed a moment later by Locke.

"Alex, are you alright?" his mom said, rushing past the others and hugging him as he lay trapped in bed.

"Yes, mom, I'm fine, I'm fine," he assured her. "Only don't touch the left side of my head. It's still kinda sore."

"And don't drink this water over here," Tom said, motioning towards the shelf where the tick had been submerged. "It's got a dead bug in it."

"So, what happened back in the forest?" Alex asked once his mom had stopped fussing over him and Sol and Tom had untied the leather band binding him to the bed.

"We were surprised by some soldiers patrolling the borders around Hope," Locke explained. "They shouted at us to surrender but before I could say anything, Harriet had grabbed her rifle and fired on them. The bullet struck one of their laz-rifles, disarming one of their soldiers."

"The other soldiers were about to fire on Harriet," Alex's mom added, taking up the story. "And so I ... well, I ran in front of her."

"Which was very brave of you, Liz," Locke said, smiling gently at her.

"Too smeckin' right. You were amazing, Mrs. F.," Tom added admiringly.

"So they shot you?" Alex asked.

"Yes. They were aiming at Harriet, I guess. Anyway, it turns out their weapons were set to stun, so I was always going to be fine."

"You didn't look fine yesterday," Alex said, his mind conjuring unbidden a vivid image of his mom's ashen face and the smoke rising from her clothes as she lay unmoving on the forest floor.

"Even stun weapons can hurt, especially the larger caliber laz-rifles," Locke explained. "And then you arrived on the scene, closely followed by Iggy and Abby. Where had you been, by the way?"

"Oh, we were nearby ... um ... talking," Alex replied, reddening. He glanced furtively in Abby's direction, but to his disappointment she was no longer in the room.

"Right," said Locke, with a knowing look in his eyes Alex found both unsettling and irritating. "You, too, were brave, Alex, although I do wish you'd surrendered. It would have saved you that knock on the head, for one."

"I didn't know their guns were set to stun. I couldn't take the chance," Alex replied defensively. He was still feeling very angry at Locke for what had happened the night before.

"I understand," Locke said.

"So what happened after they captured you all? After I was knocked out?" Alex asked, looking at his friends rather than Locke.

"They brought us to Hope, blindfolded," Tom replied excitedly. "First they put us in a cabin and locked us in overnight. Then we had the trial this morning."

"Trial?"

"Yeah, a real trial like we used to watch on our MeChips sometimes. There was a jury and everything. It was *uber* fun!" Tom gushed.

"Fun? We could have ended up in prison permanently, you dexter," Sol said in his usual deadpan tone, looking askance at his friend and rolling his eyes.

"Prison? No way! Not once these guys took the stand. You were awesome, by the way, Dr. L. So were you, Mrs. F. I could see the mayor nodding along when you explained what had happened back in Lincoln. You had her in the palm of your hand. She believed you totally."

"Thank you, Tom," said Alex's mom, smiling at him.

"Your dad was great, too, Alex," Tom added carelessly. "Oh, I mean, not your dad, but ... um ... the man who ..." Tom trailed off, his face reddening.

"Yes, but now we should let Alex rest," Locke cut in, looking sternly at Tom from under beetling brows.

"I'll stay a few more minutes if I may, John?" Alex's mom asked.

"Of course, Liz," Locke nodded. As the old man led the two boys from the room, Alex distinctly heard Sol mutter "You are a total dexter, Tom. Do you know that?" before the door closed shut behind them.

"Are you alright, Alex?" his mom asked, coming and sitting at the end of the bed the instant the others had gone, and looking at him with real concern.

"Not really, Mom," he sighed. "The injury isn't too bad," he added, gingerly pressing his fingers to the side of his head. "But it's all this other stuff. All these secrets that are coming out. My dad and Abby's dad and the news about so many kids dying. And then there's Locke. He knew all about dad! What else is he keeping from us?"

"I don't know, Alex," his mom replied slowly. "But I do know he's doing his best. Even he's not perfect, you know."

"You don't say," Alex replied sarcastically.

"Just be patient with him. John Locke is doing what he thinks is right. We all are."

"By which you mean you and ... and ... that man?"

"Yes, Alex. But you should call him Ben."

"That's not even his real name!" Alex protested, sitting up in bed.

"It's the only name he has, Alex. The only one he remembers."

They lapsed into silence before Alex's mom eventually spoke again.

"Alex, I don't expect you to treat Ben like a father or anything, but you should know he's suffering as much as any of us. He didn't choose any of this, either. For my sake, please try not to make him feel any worse."

"So what happens next? Now we're no longer prisoners," Alex asked, changing the subject.

"There's going to be some sort of meeting tonight. All the town's leaders will be there. Locke intends to ask them to help us with our plans to defeat the MeChip."

"Are we invited?"

"Of course! But now you should rest, Alex. Tonight's going to be important. We'll all want our wits about us."

25 | Tom Bombs

Having slept the entire afternoon, Alex awoke feeling rested and refreshed. Sure, his head still ached a little and he'd have a bruise there for a few days, but the young medic Leah Mecon declared him fit to leave the tiny hospital. His friends, Sol and Tom, had taken him to a small cabin set aside for them, reunited him with his guitar—which had somehow survived the fight in the forest—then shown him to a communal bathroom where he'd enjoyed his first hot shower in over a week; a wonderful experience after so many days without any creature comforts. He'd emerged revived and invigorated, wearing clothes provided by the locals: brown corduroy pants and a green sweater that were old-fashioned but clean and comfortable.

"We won't win any fashion contests in these things," joked Tom, who was dressed the same way, as his friend reentered their cabin.

"Who cares?" Sol said, shaking his head. "I'm just glad to not be wearing the same socks I've had on this past week."

"We're all glad about that, Sol," Tom said, smirking. "I mean, I didn't want to say anything, Sol, but those feet of yours ... sheesh!" he said, waving his hand in front of his nose as if fending off a bad odor.

"You're a fine one to talk, Tom. Sharing a tent with you has been like co-habiting with a skunk that's really let itself go. And don't get me started on your dental hygiene."

Alex smiled to himself as his two friends continued bickering good-naturedly. It almost felt like the old days as they left the cabin and stepped out into the darkness.

"What's this place like?" Alex asked curiously. He hadn't seen Hope yet during the day and could make out little of it now in the dim glow cast by a handful of soft electric lights hanging from wooden posts. As they walked along a wide, straight dirt trail, he could just make out the dim shapes of wooden buildings to left and right, some shadowy trees scattered here and there, and a canopy of leaves obscuring the sky above.

"It's actually pretty stellar," Tom said, nodding. "Everything seems to be made from nature; the buildings and stuff. Not like Lincoln at all. But you'll see for yourself tomorrow. Oh, here we are."

A large edifice loomed out of the darkness as Alex heard voices and, a moment later, saw the shadowy movement of people up ahead. A thin streak of light pierced the gloomy curtain of night as someone opened a door, illuminating at least a dozen folks milling around an entryway. Two armed soldiers flanked the path. Sol, Tom, and Alex joined the crowd as they shuffled inside a dimly-lit interior, following a short corridor that turned right, then left. A second interior entrance was ahead, this one blocked by a curtain. Someone in front of them pulled it back and a broad beam of brightness broke through, blinding Alex. He held up a hand to shield his eyes, following Tom and Sol as they walked through this second entrance.

There was movement and luminosity and noise. Before his eyes could fully recover, he was aware of the buzz of voices—of many people talking all at once. Unlike the murky corridor, this room was dazzling, with bright electric bulbs in the ceiling and along the walls. Alex blinked once, twice, and rubbed his eyes for good measure. Finally, his vision cleared and he could see what was in front of him.

It was a large hall, almost as big as the auditorium at school although not so cavernous, with wooden walls and a low ceiling. Row upon row of seats, many already occupied by townspeople, stretched out in front of him, ending before a small, raised stage at the far end. Many eyes turned to look at them as they entered, which only increased the muttering.

Feeling awkward, Alex scanned the crowd in search of a friendly face but couldn't make out a single member of his group among the throng. With the advantage of his extra height, however, Tom was more successful.

"Over here," he urged, nudging Alex and nodding to the left.

"Who is it?" Alex asked, still scanning the crowd as Tom led them forward.

"Your friend Leah the medic."

"She's not my friend," Alex replied, reddening as he finally spotted her about halfway towards the front and standing by the wall. She was still wearing her medical scrubs and appeared to be staring eagerly at the stage, on which several people were already gathered.

"Not your friend? Well, she should be. I mean, look at her. Tidy, no? And smart, too, I bet," Tom speculated, grinning broadly.

"What makes you say that?"

"Well, she's gonna be a doctor. That takes brains."

"You know what? I'm going to look for the others," Alex said, feeling oddly reluctant to engage with Leah right now and casting a glance around the room once more.

"Really? Suit yourself. But I'm gonna say hi. I want to ask her how many brain cells you lost with that bruise there," he said, winking at Alex before continuing to make his way through the crowd.

"There he goes on his never-ending mission to make a dexter out of himself with every girl he meets," Sol observed, shaking his head solemnly.

"At least he's trying," Alex said. "When did you last—"

"Me? I don't have to try, Alex, I've already—"

"Already what?" Alex asked curiously.

"Hey, there are the others," Sol said, pointing up towards the front and avoiding Alex's gaze.

They made their way through the press of people, finally reaching their friends. Everyone else was there except Iggy. Harriet greeted Sol with a smile and immediately engaged him in an animated conversation about some musical gear she'd found backstage. Meanwhile, Alex's mom hugged her son.

"You look better already," she said, scrutinizing him carefully, a hand on each of his shoulders as she pulled back and looked him up and down. "And that sweater really suits you. I always said you should wear green more often."

"Thanks, Mom," Alex replied, glancing at the others. He tried to catch Abby's eye but she was chatting with Locke while casting occasional glances towards the far side of the hall in the direction of Leah Mecon. Alex wondered if she was still thinking about the embarrassing scene in the hospital earlier.

"Where's Thomas?" Alex's mom asked, looking around.

Alex was about to respond when Tom himself appeared from behind a group of locals.

"Right here, Mrs. F.," he said.

"Are you alright?" Alex asked his friend, who was red in the face and scowling.

"I'm fine," he said, hastily rearranging his features into an unconvincing smile, his voice sounding strained and oddly high-pitched as his eyes flickered from Alex to his mom and then away into the crowd.

But a moment later, when Liz had turned around to chat with Alice and Susanna, the mask-like smile slipped away and Tom's grimace returned. "I'm not fine, though," he said in an angry undertone only Alex could hear.

"Why? What happened?"

"*He* did," Tom spat bitterly.

"What? Who?"

"Him. Iggy. Interrupted me just when I was getting started with Leah. Look," he instructed, glaring back at where he'd just been. Alex craned his neck and caught sight of Iggy. He was leaning against the far wall chatting comfortably with Leah, who was looking up at him. At first, it appeared to Alex as if she was frowning and he wondered if Iggy had offended her. But then her face broke into a smile and she uncrossed her arms and casually ran her fingers through her hair.

"It's not enough that he has Abby and flirts with Sybil all the smeckin' time. Does he really have to move in on the new girl, too? He even made a joke about my drumming," Tom said, adding some swear words Alex was pretty sure would have got his friend expelled if they'd been back at school.

"Just what the smeck do they see in that no-good braggster?" Tom continued, glowering. "Alright, so he's good-looking and a great musician. And I guess he is the star quarterback and his grades are decent. But what does that matter when he's so arrogant?" Tom asked angrily.

"No idea, Tom," Alex said, not sure what to say. "Maybe some girls are superficial and like that kind of stuff," Alex ventured at last.

"Who's superficial?" a voice asked as Alex wheeled round.

It was Abby.

"Oh, no one. We were just ..." Tom replied, trailing off.

"I think I know what you were just—" she began, looking in the direction of Iggy and Leah. But before she could say more a loud bell rang out, bringing the crowd instantly to silence.

On the stage stood a middle-aged woman. She was wearing a green robe and a wide, welcoming smile. Her arms were outstretched, palms open to the audience. Her copper-colored hair was graying around the temples, while her green eyes were bright and penetrating.

"Welcome all of you," she declared, beaming as her eyes flitted across the crowd. "I am Jane Mecon, Mayor of Hope, and I call to order this 950th meeting of our town."

26 | Locke's Entreaty

"We have gathered to discuss the arrival of visitors from Lincoln and to consider their request for help," said the mayor once everyone was seated. "Their leader, Dr. John Locke, has asked to speak to us," she continued, motioning for him to come on stage. A technician handed the old man a microphone as he gazed out at the crowd. Looking over his shoulder at the sea of faces, Alex guessed there must be at least 500 people present.

"Thank you, Mayor Mecon, and all you good people of Hope for granting us sanctuary. Thank you also for agreeing to listen to our plea for help," Locke began. "What we are asking is no small thing. Our goal is nothing less than to defeat the MeChip. We have discovered a weakness which, if exploited, could free every single American from its evil grip. But we need you. Only with your support can we do this. You alone possess the power to change our country's future—to make history."

The crowd listened in silence as Locke told his story. He spoke slowly and clearly, repeating much of what Alex already knew: of Locke's creation of the MeChip two decades earlier, his growing fears over its misuse, his fall from power, and his discovery of the MeChip's vulnerability to music. He told them of his plan to defeat the MeChip, of his capture by General Arnold before he could act, of Alex's actions on the night of the Best Band contest, and of the destruction of the MeChips of everyone who had heard Alex, Sol and Tom's performance. Finally, he described the attack by the Regulators, the escape to the forest, and their quest to find Hope.

"Now that we know the right music works and can defeat the MeChip, we need everyone to hear it. I have developed a program that can hack into the MeChip control stations. Once I use it, we can broadcast to the entire nation and break the MeChips of every single American under its thrall. But I need your help acquiring the right equipment, as mine was lost back in Lincoln. Will you help us? Will you help your country?"

"Thank you, Dr. Locke. That is a lot to absorb," said the mayor after a lengthy pause. "Does anyone wish to ask anything of our guest?"

They did. For almost two hours the crowd interrogated Locke, peppering him with question after question as they sought to understand more fully what he was proposing and how his plan might work. Locke answered every query and concern convincingly and in detail.

In spite of his anger at Locke for keeping so many secrets, Alex was impressed once more at the old man's intelligence and composure. As Alex scanned the crowd, he saw some of them nodding as Locke made his case for why the town should help them. But many remained impassive, their features hard to decipher, while a few were openly shaking their heads in disbelief or opposition.

"Thank you for your thorough and, I believe, honest answers," the mayor said at last. "Under normal circumstances, we would now put the matter to a vote. Yet this issue is so important, and the consequences so far-reaching, we all need time to sleep on it before we decide. I therefore propose to close our meeting and resume tomorrow at 7 p.m. sharp."

So that was it, Alex thought as they retraced their steps out of the crowded hall, the buzz of voices all around them. They would know their fate—and perhaps the fate of their country—tomorrow night.

27 | Electa's Tour

"Wake up, dexter!"

Alex rubbed his eyes, yawned and, with an effort, sat up in bed. Tom was standing over him and shaking his head, his broad grin—genuine this time—firmly back in place.

"What time is it?" Alex groaned, yawning once more.

"Nearly ten. Dude, you totally slept in. Missed breakfast."

"Really?" Alex said despondently as his stomach emitted an odd grumbling sound.

"Don't worry, I got you this." Tom placed something on the bedside table. "Enjoy. These people really know how to bake!" he said enthusiastically.

Alex glanced down. There on a plate was a piece of bread layered with what appeared to be honey. It didn't look like much to Alex. Just a standard slice, a bit thicker than he was used to but nothing out of the ordinary. He picked it up and gingerly took a small bite while Tom looked on, still grinning.

"Wow. This is really good," Alex admitted, surprised at how fresh and delicious it tasted.

"I told you! Anyways, you should get up. They're giving us a tour of the town in a few minutes. And the girl who's leading it is smeckin' tidy!"

"Welcome to Hope, everyone. I'm Electa Gage and I'm going to show you around the town—your new home now you have been granted sanctuary. Follow me, please."

"See, I told you she was tidy," Tom whispered, smirking as he nudged Alex and Sol, who simply rolled his eyes and shook his head. Alex could see what Tom meant, though. Electa Gage was tall with straight, coal-black hair and large, almond-shaped eyes. He guessed she was a year older than them, maybe two.

"Don't even think about it. She's too old for you," Sol muttered as they walked slowly along with the others and Tom continued to gaze admiringly at Electa.

"You think so? I'm not—"

"If you look to your left, you'll see our school," Electa said, causing Tom to stop mid-sentence as she pointed to a large, low, wooden structure.

"How many students does it have?" Sybil asked.

"An excellent question. About 150," Electa said, smiling for the first time.

"What's the age range?" Sybil added.

"Another great question! They start at five and go through to eighteen. We also have childcare for the younger kids," Electa replied, before leading them on to the next sight.

"So, what do you think?" Tom asked as the three friends sat down for dinner in the town's busy communal cafeteria.

"You were right," Alex admitted. "It's *uber* cool here. I love the way they've used the natural resources all around them—wood for all the buildings, growing their own food, using heat pumps to warm their buildings and the nearby river for—"

"Yeah, and the way they've hidden themselves from prying eyes—low buildings under the trees, no connection to the outside world. The place really blends into the woods—it almost feels like a living part of the ecosystem," Sol agreed.

"I always thought off-gridders were crazy, but I can't disagree with you, Sol my friend. I think I'll have to change my mind about them," Tom said, chuckling.

"And I always thought you chipslaves were nuts, too, but ... well, I'm still on the fence about that one," came a voice from behind them.

The three of them whirled around. It was Leah. She was holding a tray of food and wore the ghost of a smile.

"Hi, Leah! Would you like to join us?" Tom asked enthusiastically.

"I guess I—"

"Leah. Leah. Over here!" interrupted a voice. The group turned and saw Electa Gage. She was sitting with Sybil and Iggy at a table on the far side of the cafeteria and waving enthusiastically at Leah.

"Oh, that's my friend Electa. I'd better go join her," Leah said, turning and walking to the other side of the room.

"Iggy again!" Tom said, scowling. "And now he's got Leah, Electa, and Sybil all to himself."

"Here's something that'll cheer you up, Tom," Sol said between mouthfuls of food. "Harriet was telling me they have loads of great music gear backstage of the main hall: amps, mikes, guitars, synths, even drum kits."

But Tom didn't reply. He was still glaring in Iggy's direction, his hands gripping the side of the table, his food untouched.

"Is the gear old or new?" Alex asked.

"Old, I think. But we can take a look after the meeting."

"Speaking of which, we should finish up. It's almost seven already," Alex said, looking at an old-fashioned clock on the wall.

"Yeah, let's go discover our fate," Sol said, frowning as he wolfed down his food.

28 | Mayor Mecon's Message

"We are here to decide if we should grant Dr. Locke's request for our help in his fight against the MeChip," Mayor Mecon commenced as the final stragglers entered the hall. "You have heard his words, asked him many questions, and had time to reflect on his answers. I would like to put the matter to a full town vote tonight. Before I do so, however, tradition dictates that anyone who wishes to speak should be heard. Does anyone have an opinion they would like to share?"

One of the half-dozen people sitting onstage raised her hand. She looked familiar and for a moment Alex wondered if he'd seen her around the town that day during Electa's tour. Then she stood up and Alex remembered exactly where he'd encountered her before. She was the leader of the patrol they'd fought two days earlier. Dressed in military fatigues, she had graying, shoulder-length hair and steely-gray eyes. A laser pistol was holstered in her belt.

"Captain Bailey, you have the floor," the mayor said, handing her the microphone.

"Thank you. I'll keep this short and simple. Everyone knows how much I hate the MeChip. It has blighted the country I love. But my duty is to the town of Hope. This scheme is too risky. Too many things could go wrong. What if it fails and the Fixers trace it back to us? And even if it succeeds, do you really expect President Davison and her thugs to give up without a fight? This plan puts everything we've worked for here at risk. It places all of us—men, women, and children—in danger. I will vote no."

She handed the microphone back and sat down, leaning towards an elderly man on her right and whispering in his ear. He nodded vigorously and he wasn't the only one. There was a muttering throughout the crowd, a scattered round of applause, and several shouts of "Hear, Hear!" It was obvious more than a few shared her opinion.

"Thank you, Captain Bailey," said Mayor Mecon. "Anyone else?"

Several others spoke. All echoed Captain Bailey's sentiments, repeating her concerns for the safety of Hope. Alex noticed the speakers were all older. All expressed fears for the town's children if the plan failed. Finally, a younger member of the audience raised her hand.

"Yes, Electa, please let us know your thoughts," Mayor Mecon said, smiling at the tall teenager as she strode to the front of the hall and took the mike.

"We've heard from our respected elders," said Electa, her voice confident and clear as she nodded towards Captain Bailey. "You said you're worried about our town and especially our younger inhabitants. Dr. Locke's plan puts us at risk, you say. But aren't we already at risk? Isn't every day a risk when President Davison and her cronies run this country? For all we know, they could already be planning to destroy our town. I believe we will never be safe until the MeChip is defeated once and for all. And I am not alone in this. Many of my friends feel the same way. Dr. Locke has offered us a chance to take the fight to our enemies rather than hiding here in the forest. We may never get another opportunity. That is why I will vote yes—yes to freedom, yes to democracy, yes to justice!" she concluded, raising a loud cheer from the teenagers and twenty-somethings in the crowd.

"She gets to vote?" Alex asked Sol over the noise.

"Yeah. She told us that during the tour, weren't you listening? This is a participatory democracy, meaning everyone gets to have a say in any major decisions. And they believe youth should have a voice, so the voting age is fifteen."

"*Uber* cool."

More young people addressed the crowd, supporting Electa and confirming they, too, would vote in favor of Locke's request. Alex noticed Leah standing next to Electa by the wall, although she didn't speak.

After that a few older people took the microphone. Some seemed to have been persuaded by Electa's eloquence, while others continued to support Captain Bailey.

"Anyone else?" Mayor Mecon asked after more than an hour, her eyes searching the hall. No one raised their hand.

"What do *you* think, Mayor?" came a shout from the back. The cry was taken up by others from around the room.

Jane Mecon took several seconds to answer.

"As Mayor of Hope, I confess I am unsure," she began, speaking slowly, almost cautiously, as if weighing every word. "Captain Bailey is right that this venture brings risk to our town. So far, we seem to have escaped detection—or at least the interest—of those who run our country. Helping Dr. Locke may put us in peril, especially if this plan does not succeed," she said, before pausing.

Alex realized he was holding his breath, waiting for her to say more. Mayor Mecon looked down at the ground for so long Alex thought her speech was finished. But there was more.

"These are the fears of someone charged with leading our town—our refuge from danger, our calm in the storm. They are the fears of a leader and a mother. But as someone who loves my country—as someone who cares about our fellow citizens whether they are near or far—I believe we should do whatever we can to help Dr. Locke and his friends," she said at last, looking back at the crowd, her eyes meeting theirs as her voice rang out true and clear.

"These brave people are fighting for democracy—something we pride ourselves on here in Hope. They are fighting for equality and fairness, for truth and freedom. These are things we stand for, things Hope stands for. They are the ideals our country was founded upon.

How can we *not* support them in their quest to free our fellow Americans? How can we *not* help them defeat the evil that inhabits the White House? You ask what I think, friends? I say I will vote to join their cause. I will vote yes."

There was silence. Captivated by her charisma, no one spoke, no one moved, for several long seconds.

Then the hall exploded as the audience roared its approval, whooping and cheering and applauding their inspirational leader.

The vote was a walkover: 407 votes in favor to just 55 against.

"Thank you for voting, friends. Tomorrow the work must begin. But tonight let us celebrate this decision," Mayor Mecon announced as the noise died down. "Who would like to have some music? I for one am eager to hear this vaunted band of which Dr. Locke has spoken so highly and on which our future hopes lie. Will you play for us, Alex?" she asked, turning to look at the stunned teenager.

29 | Xander and the Plan A's

Twenty minutes later and Alex, Tom, and Sol were onstage with instruments hooked up to amps and speakers as they ran a sound check.

Sol had been right about the gear, Alex thought to himself. It was *uber* cool. It turned out Electa Gage was a gifted musician—she played keys—and she'd helped them backstage, showing them the best equipment. Now she was offstage with a mixing desk, twiddling nobs and pressing buttons to help them get the best sound. While the others were setting up, Alex had rushed back to the cabin and grabbed his X-shaped guitar—the instrument he'd brought with him all the way from Lincoln. Now it was hooked up to a large amp, tuned and ready to play.

Alex looked out at the crowd. A few of the older folks had left but the rest were obviously in a festive mood, drinking and laughing as they looked towards the stage or chatted with friends. Alex swallowed, trying not to think about their last gig or about how many hundreds of people were staring at him right now. He turned to Sol and Tom.

"What should we play?"

"How about 'Lift You Up?'" Sol suggested. It was a well-known Rock Shop number that had been a hit a few years ago. Upbeat and dance-worthy, they'd practiced it plenty of times and knew it well.

"Good choice," Alex nodded.

"Then let's smeckin' do this," Tom said, grinning from ear to ear. He looked at Alex. "Count us in?"

"Alright. Ready? One-two-three-four," Alex intoned, nodding with each beat as he led off on his X-shaped guitar, followed four bars later by Sol on bass, then by Tom's smashing drums. Finally, the vocals entered the mix:

> *"We are here, we are young,*
> *We are true, to this song,*
> *Just can't wait,*
> *To lift you up tonight*
> *We will try, and we'll win,*
> *Don't you fight, just give in,*
> *And join us,*
> *As we lift you up tonight..."*

Already the crowd were dancing and cheering as Alex launched into the next verse, trying not to grin. The second song went even better, while for the third Alex had a sudden inspiration to invite Abby to join them on an Ultralux Synthi-Piano he'd seen backstage. At first she shook her head vigorously, looking distinctly uncomfortable. But when Alex asked a second time, and when Sol and Tom joined in, smiling encouragingly, she finally agreed and strode onstage.

She aced the number, adding an awesome impromptu solo during the breakdown that had the crowd cheering louder than ever and adding texture and life to the next three songs as well. Finally, after playing half-a-dozen tunes, Alex held up his hands in gratitude.

"Thanks, everyone. We are Xander and the Plan A's, with special guest star Abby Adams on keys. That's all from us—thank you!"

"What? No way," Tom protested from behind the drums.

"Always leave them wanting more, remember?" Alex said, turning away from the mike and laughing. "Besides, there are some other great musicians here," he added, nodding towards Iggy and Harriet, who were standing off to one side. Harriet was cheering and whooping, while Iggy had his arms crossed and was scowling, staring off into the crowd.

"Don't worry, the party's not over," Alex said, turning back to the mike and speaking to the crowd again. "We have some other awesome musicians from Lincoln here tonight. Iggy Elgar is lead singer and guitarist in last year's Best Band winner, *Iggy and the Overlords*, while our friend Harriet's band *Saratoga Redux* finished as runners-up. Perhaps we can persuade them to come on up and play something? Let's hear it for Iggy and Harriet!"

The crowd started cheering their names. Iggy frowned, arms still crossed. But at the sound of his name being chanted by hundreds of enthusiastic new fans, he finally relented, a smirk drawing slowly across his handsome face. As Harriet jumped onstage and Sol passed her the bass guitar, Electa took over the Synthi-Piano from Abby, while a friend of Electa's sat down at the drum stool just vacated by Tom. Meanwhile, Iggy sauntered onstage and held up a hand to acknowledge the crowd.

"Thanks for warming them up, Franklin," Iggy muttered to Alex in his usual, arrogant drawl. "Now for some real music!"

Same old Iggy, Alex thought as he stepped back into the crowd. Still, tonight Alex didn't care. He was too happy with his performance, too delighted to be playing music again, and too thrilled with the crowd's reaction to worry about his rival.

He wove his way slowly through the cheering crowd to the side of the hall where he found an empty seat and dropped into it, tired but elated. Curious to see how the new band did, he watched as Iggy started his first song. Alex knew from experience that it often took some time for musicians who had never played together before to really gel. He wondered if they'd chosen a good tune, how talented the drummer was, and if Harriet and Iggy would perform well together.

He needn't have worried. The foursome had chosen a Thrashtech number all of them obviously knew well. Iggy instantly won over the audience with his power chords on guitar as Harriet laid down a brilliant throbbing beat on bass, Electa chimed in on keys, and the young woman on drums nailed down the rhythm section.

Satisfied, Alex scanned the crowd. He saw his mother and Ben—or whoever the man really was—dancing near the front. Both were smiling. Tom was nearby trying to talk with Sybil, who was tapping her feet and clapping to the music, but looked like she couldn't catch half of what he was saying over the noise of the band. Meanwhile, Sol had taken over the mixing desk from Electa and was nodding approvingly in time with the beat. Even Locke looked as if he was enjoying himself as he danced with Mayor Mecon, his face occasionally cracking into a wry smile. Susanna and Alice were in the crowd too, swaying to the sound and cheering.

But where was Abby? For a moment he wondered if she'd left. Then he spotted her. She was making her way through the audience towards him. She caught his eye, smiled, and then stopped, frowned, and turned away, much to Alex's confusion. Before he could wonder what had happened, though, someone sat down next to him and started speaking.

"Nice set, tick boy."

Alex turned and looked into two penetrating green eyes.

"Um ... thanks, Leah," he said. "Do you mean it?"

"Yeah, I mean it! You guys were great. I mean, *uber* great! I have to admit, I thought you chipslaves were good for nothing. I may have to change my mind."

"Um ... thanks?" Alex replied, feeling a little confused.

"What's up? You look like I just asked you a tough algebra question," she said, frowning.

"Well, it's just you were all serious in the hospital when I first arrived and now you're being ... I don't know ... different."

"I'm *working* at the hospital, learning my trade. And there are lives at stake. I take it seriously, you know? Here, I can just enjoy myself."

"Okay, I get it," Alex said, nodding. "Can I ask you a question?"

"Sure."

"Why didn't you say anything at the meeting just now? I mean, Electa spoke up for us and some of her friends, too, but you didn't. Do you think they were wrong to support us?"

"No, not at all," she said, laughing. "It's mostly because of my mom,"

"Your mom?"

"Yeah, the one who looks like me only older? Who has the same surname?"

"What? Who?"

"The mayor, you dexter!" she said, laughing. "My mom's the mayor. I prefer to leave the politics to her. Medicine's my thing. Anyway, Electa was so *uber* articulate I don't think I could have added anything."

"Oh, right," Alex said, feeling foolish for not putting two-and-two together and realizing Leah and Mayor Mecon shared not only the same surname, but the same DNA.

"Now can I ask you a question?" Leah asked back.

"Sure, I guess," Alex replied.

"What's the deal with you and Iggy?"

"What do you mean?"

"Well, I can tell he doesn't like you and I'm guessing the feeling's mutual. What's the story?"

"Oh, that. Well, it would take too long to tell. Plus, I'm in a good mood right now and I don't want to ruin it by dredging up the past."

"Fine. Keep your secrets then. But I'll find out eventually," she said, arching an eyebrow and smiling enigmatically as she stood up and walked back into the crowd to join a group of girlfriends dancing and singing to the music.

30 | Plans and Schemes

Alex woke up smiling. For a millisec, he couldn't remember why. Then it all came flooding back. They were going to help. The people of Hope were joining their quest to beat the MeChip. What's more, the party last night had been fun. Alex had danced along to a bunch of great songs, laughing and cheering with Tom, Sol, Leah, Sybil and the rest as Harriet and the others crushed it onstage. The only disappointment was he hadn't seen Abby again. Still, he was sure he'd catch up with her today. Everything was going to be alright. He just knew it. Still smiling, he climbed out of bed and started to dress.

The meeting lasted a long time. At first, Alex listened attentively, hanging on every word as Hope's leaders and John Locke discussed the plan and how to make it a success. But as time wore on Alex's attention gradually began to wander. He knew what Mayor Mecon, Dr. Locke, Captain Bailey, and the others were saying was important. But it was technical and hard to follow as they analyzed and debated every aspect of the emerging idea.

He wasn't alone. As the talk grew more detailed, Tom nodded off at one point, his head slumping onto his chest and then rotating gently to rest against Alex's shoulder for at least 10 minutes until he suddenly jerked awake with a snort, staring wide-eyed around him, his mouth hanging open for several seconds until he realized where he was. Meanwhile, Sybil was staring off into the middle distance and distractedly chewing on the ends of her long red hair, her thoughts clearly elsewhere.

Alex's attention returned briefly when they talked about the music. But a lot of it he already knew, as Locke explained to Hope's leaders how only genuine, "real" instruments would work and only the finest music would break the MeChip's control.

After seven hours they finally had a plan. Their first step would be to get hold of the right equipment—software and hardware—for Locke to hack into the MeChip's central mainframe. They also needed gear that would allow them to direct the satellites that sent signals to the MeChips and to the local control stations based around the country. This apparatus was not especially uncommon or hard to acquire—it was clearly Locke's skill that was rare rather than the tools he needed. Still, they did not have what they needed in Hope. Instead, a small group of them would need to go to the nearest city—a place called Fairview about fifteen miles away.

Once they had the gear, Locke and a couple of locals who understood coding and hardware would get to work on setting it up on top of a nearby hill overlooking Hope. There was an old observatory that would serve as a broadcasting station for their music. With any luck, they'd be able to get things set up within a few weeks.

Meantime, Alex, Tom, and Sol would work on the music. They'd be joined by Abby, since Locke felt after last night's performance that having a keyboard in the mix could only strengthen the music's effect on people's MeChips.

While these preparations were underway Mayor Mecon, Captain Bailey and Locke would also be developing a plan for what would happen after America's MeChips were disabled, including how to rapidly communicate with other secret groups scattered around the country who might be able to help them topple the government once the revolution began—and how they might get the Regs and others on their side.

"So, step one is to visit Fairview," Mayor Mecon reiterated as the meeting wrapped up.

"When should we go?" asked Locke.

"What do you think, Captain Bailey?" asked Mayor Mecon, turning to Hope's military commander.

"If we're really going to do this then there's no time like the present. Our vehicles are ready to roll and we know what we need. I say we go tomorrow."

31 | Neil's Music Emporium

Alex pulled the brim of his baseball cap a little lower and scanned the crowd. It felt *uber* weird being back in a city again.

Fairview wasn't even that big—he guessed it was about the size of his hometown of Lincoln. But after so many days in the forest it felt massive, like MePics Alex had seen of New York or New Tokyo. He took a deep breath, watching the people walking and talking and laughing all the way down Main Street. They were wearing their MeChips, of course. How else would this place—which to Alex looked disheveled and dirty—bring a smile to so many faces? Only that technology's rose-tinted view of the world could keep these people satisfied with such squalor.

"Come on dexter, what are you waiting for?" Iggy said, nodding at the blinking green figure on the traffic lights and poking him in the ribs as he stepped out onto the crosswalk.

Trying to suppress his irritation Alex followed, trotting to keep up with the older boy's longer stride. Why did he have to get paired up with Iggy, of all people? He knew it was because the two of them would make the best choices when it came to mike cables and other gear they needed for their guitars and vocals. But knowing this didn't make Alex any happier.

There were only seven of them on the mission: Locke, Iggy, Alex, Captain Bailey, and three other townsfolk from Hope. Iggy and Alex would see to the musical side, while the three folks from Hope would buy the electronic gear and other hardware Locke said was needed. Meanwhile, Locke would stay out of sight by the vehicles, ready to check the gear as it was brought back from the shops, and Captain

Bailey would stay with him, on hand in case of any trouble, her two laser pistols close to hand.

They'd headed into town in two aging pickup trucks.

"Have you been here before?" Alex asked as they drove down an old dirt road that led out of the forest.

"Sure. We come in about once a month," Captain Bailey replied, glancing at him through the rear-view mirror and raising her voice so he could hear her over the noise of the engine. "Hope isn't fully self-sustaining yet. We still need supplies from time to time—medicines, plant seeds, and stuff like that.

"Is it always you who goes?"

"Mostly we send Dave; the guy driving the other pickup. The shopkeepers seem to like him well enough. They think he has a farm way up the valley."

"So there's not much danger for you in Fairview?"

"I wouldn't say that. We just try not to draw too much attention to ourselves, is all."

"And what about us? Me and Iggy and Dr. Locke."

"What about you?"

"What if ... I don't know ... the Fixers are reading people's thoughts or something? Could they recognize us?"

"You're safe on that score, Alex," John Locke chimed in. "MeChips can implant ideas and images *into* your brain and they can receive various simple mental instructions you give them, but they can't take all your thoughts *out*—they're not mind readers," he assured Alex over the noise of the pickup engine. "So just because someone with a MeChip sees your face, that doesn't mean the Controllers know about it."

"That's true. But your photos may have been circulated on the news and they'll have security cameras on the main streets, so keep the caps on," Captain Bailey warned.

An hour later they were in Fairview and Alex was following Iggy onto the crowded crosswalk.

Like Alex, Iggy was wearing a cap pulled low over his eyes. Without looking to see if Alex was following, Iggy strode purposefully across the busy street, Alex a couple of steps behind. Within seconds they were in front of their destination—Neil's Music Emporium.

A bell jingled above the doorway as Alex and Iggy entered and a middle-aged man with watery-blue eyes and long, graying hair pulled back in a ponytail looked up from behind the counter of an otherwise empty shop.

"Can I help you?" he asked without much enthusiasm.

"Mike cables," Iggy said, stepping forward.

"First aisle on the left," the man replied, nodding towards the far corner of the store. Iggy and Alex wandered over and started searching. There were several different brands but they were looking in particular for a classic cable they felt would work best with a genuine, antique microphone. At first, Alex thought they wouldn't find anything useful: the place only seemed to have new cables designed to go with the latest synthi-mikes. Finally, though, Iggy found an old lead at the back of the bottom shelf. He held it up, blew the dust off it, and smiled.

Next, they searched for guitar strings. Once more, they were looking for the older variety. Again, they were in luck, finally finding them tucked away behind the newer synthi-plas brands.

"Looks like we have what we need. Let's get out of here," Iggy muttered under his breath. Alex nodded, breathing a sigh of relief. It had been easy in the end. They'd found what they needed. Now they could go. Mission accomplished.

They were about to make their way to the counter when the bell over the shop door jingled again and more customers entered the shop.

Alex's eyes darted towards the entrance and he caught his breath. For these were no ordinary customers.

They were Regs.

32 | Iggy's Lies

There were two of them. One was tall, probably in his early forties, his partner younger, shorter, with her hair tied back in a bun. They were in standard Regulator gear, from the peaked cap with its silver eagle button on the front, to the black leather jacket with light gray epaulets on each shoulder, down to the tall leather boots. Each had a baton and pair of handcuffs hanging from their belt, with the standard-issue Mark 2 laser pistol nestled in its holster.

Alex froze. Could he escape? Slowly he started to lower himself below the Regs' line of sight and behind the shelf, when Iggy grabbed his arm and pulled him upright.

"What are you doing?" hissed the older boy. "Stay calm. Follow my lead." Immediately, Iggy started looking at the shelves, picking up items and putting them back again as if he was still searching for something. Taking a deep breath, Alex did the same while watching the Regs from the corner of his vision.

Meanwhile, the Regs were at the counter.

"Hey Neil, how are you? Business good?" asked the male Reg.

"Not complaining," the shopkeeper replied. "You?"

"Been better, Neil. We got dragged into that business in Lincoln the other week. You know, the school auditorium fire. What a mess!"

"Was it arson, like that general said on the news?"

"Looks like it."

"Caught the guy who did it?"

"Locke? Not yet. But it's only a matter of time."

"I hope so. He sounds like a nasty piece of work."

"You don't know the half of it," the Reg said, shaking his head bitterly.

"What do you mean?" Neil asked, leaning forward on the counter.

"You can add kidnapping and murder to his rap sheet."

"You don't say."

"Yup. It'll be the chair for him when he's caught."

"No more than he deserves," declared Neil, nodding his head slowly. "Anyhoo, the good news is I got a delivery of the new amps I told you about. Wanna take a look?"

"Sure do," the Reg replied enthusiastically.

"Wait here, I'll fetch one."

Neil disappeared into a back room, returning moments later with a small amp. It was shiny and new, with plasti-tube framing and the words "HCA Amp 54" emblazoned in silver along the side.

"Nice!" said the Reg.

"Yup, Happy Corps has done it again," Neil said, beaming back. "Wanna try it out?" You can use this guitar here if you like."

The Reg opened his mouth to speak when his partner interrupted him.

"I thought we were only coming in for a millisec?" she said, looking distinctly unimpressed.

Her partner didn't seem to hear her, though, as he busied himself with the amp.

"I'm gonna get some lunch. I'll be in the diner when you're done. Okay?" She shook her head and rolled her eyes as he grunted a distracted answer. A moment later she had left the shop.

"Come on," Iggy whispered, elbowing Alex in the ribs. "Let's buy this stuff and get out of here."

Alex realized he'd been holding his breath. He exhaled and followed Iggy to the counter. The older boy slapped the cables and guitar strings on the counter and the shopkeeper looked up.

"Just these?" he said, most of his attention still on the Reg, who was busy hooking up the guitar to the amp.

Iggy nodded.

"That'll be—let's see—fifty-five bucks."

Iggy took out the money and laid it on the counter.

"Need a bag?"

Iggy shook his head, grabbed the gear, and made to leave.

They were almost at the door when a voice stopped them in their tracks.

"Shouldn't you kids be in school?"

They turned to see the Reg staring at them, straightening up and evidently done with hooking up the guitar to the amp.

"No school today. Teacher training," Iggy replied matter-of-factly.

"You're not from around here," the Reg said, looking at Iggy more closely. It was a statement, not a question. "Where do you live?" he said, his gaze shifting from Iggy to Alex.

"We're from—" Iggy began, but the man cut him off.

"I asked him, not you," the Reg said, still staring at Alex.

"Lincoln," Alex replied without thinking.

"You go to Lincoln High?" asked the Reg, his eyes narrowing suspiciously.

"Lincoln East," Iggy said before Alex could speak.

"Lincoln East, huh?"

Iggy nodded.

"So you wouldn't have been near Lincoln High the night of the fire?"

"No, sir," Iggy replied.

"How about you?" he said, turning his attention back to Alex.

"Who? Me?" Alex said, his heart racing.

"Yeah, you. Were you near Lincoln High on the night of the fire?"

"I was ... I was—"

"He was with me," Iggy cut in. "My annoying little brother. Can't get rid of him," he shrugged.

"And your name is ..."

"Dave Smith. And this is Andy."

Alex watched the Reg, wondering if he would use his MeChip to check their identities. But the Reg continued speaking without the momentary pause he would have needed to access the MeChip's database.

"Right. And what school do you go to again?"

"Lincoln East," Iggy replied instantly.

"And what are you doing in Fairview?"

"Vacation. Family trip," Iggy said casually.

There was a long pause as the Reg looked at them, his brow furrowed.

"Okay. You can go. But stay out of trouble," he said finally.

"Yes, sir."

The bell above the door jingled once more as Iggy pushed it open and sauntered outside, Alex just behind him.

They crossed the street and were almost two blocks away before either of them spoke: "What the smeck were you thinking, you total freakin' dexter?" Iggy asked angrily, turning to face Alex.

"What do you mean?" Alex said.

"You told them we were from Lincoln. Why didn't you lie?"

"I didn't think—"

"You can say that again. Didn't you hear them? What happened at the Best Band contest is big news. You could have got us caught," Iggy spat.

"But we weren't caught," Alex said defensively.

"No thanks to you. If I hadn't kept my cool and lied about our school we'd probably be in handcuffs by now. Smeck knows what would have happened."

There was silence as they began walking once more, continuing down Main Street and retracing their steps towards the parking lot where Captain Bailey and Dr. Locke would—or should—be waiting for them.

"Honestly, you are such a smeckin' liability," Iggy said at last. "You were no help when we got rid of the guns back in Lincoln and you were hopeless here, too."

"Hey, that's not fair, I only—"

"What Locke sees in you I have no idea," Iggy continued, cutting Alex off. "It should be *me* playing guitar when we broadcast, not you."

Iggy had stopped walking for a second time and was glaring at Alex, his lips curled derisively.

"I'm the one with the talent, everyone knows it," Iggy continued, staring hard at Alex as if daring him to disagree. "I won last year's Best Band contest while you froze. And I would have won this year if you hadn't ruined it."

"Ruined it?"

"Yeah. You and the old man with his crazy plan."

"If you think it's such a bad idea then why do you want to be involved?" Alex shot back.

"It *is* a bad idea. No question. But since I can't go back to Lincoln, someone competent should be running things so it has at least a *chance* of succeeding."

"And that someone is you?"

Iggy didn't answer. He didn't have to. His confident expression said it all.

"Look, I don't know why Locke picked me for this, but he has," Alex began. "And we just have to accept—"

But Iggy wasn't listening. He'd stopped for a third time and was staring at a shop across the street.

"I feel like some food." Without waiting for Alex's response, he stepped onto the street.

Alex paused for a millisec before rushing after him.

"What are you doing?" Alex hissed, catching up with his rival. "Captain Bailey said we should come straight back after we get the gear. No detours."

"You know what? Captain Bailey shot a laz-rifle at me in the forest and then voted to kick us out of Hope, so I don't much care what she says."

Iggy reached the other sidewalk and approached the shop, pausing for a moment to hold the door open for an attractive young woman who was leaving.

"Thanks," she smiled, eyeing Iggy with obvious interest.

"Anytime," Iggy replied casually, grinning back at her before stepping inside the store.

The door slammed in Alex's face just as he reached it. His mind was racing. They should not be doing this. He knew that. But Iggy was inside already. Should he wait out on the street or follow him? Was it better to head inside and make sure Iggy didn't get into any trouble or stand here loitering on the sidewalk?

For a millisec, he was gripped by indecision. Then he made up his mind. Reaching out, he grabbed the door handle, pushed, and stepped inside.

33 | Fran's Fooderia

Alex stood transfixed. The first thing he noticed was the smell. A delicious aroma of freshly-brewed coffee and pastries straight from the oven wafted over him.

He was in a café. It was bustling with activity as customers lined up to order or sat at tables, eating, drinking, or chatting. For a millisec he thought his MeChip had switched back on, for the place looked lovely. It was warm and welcoming, the wooden floors and table tops polished and gleaming, the décor dated but attractive. Above the counter was a hand-painted wooden sign bearing the words 'Fran's Fooderia' in loopy blue writing. Only the age of the furnishings showed Alex this wasn't a MeChip manipulation. Still, he found himself wondering how it could be so much nicer in here than outside, where the street had a dirty, disheveled look.

Alex's thoughts flashed back to the difference between John Locke's clean and tidy indie tech shop and the decay and decline just outside his doors. But Fran's Fooderia was even nicer. No wonder it was full of customers. He wondered for a moment if they saw it as he did, or whether their MeChips had conjured a more modern image?

But this wasn't the time for such musings. He stepped forward and joined Iggy in the line.

"What are you doing?" he whispered again as he drew alongside.

"What does it look like? I'm getting some food. Isn't this place great?"

"Come on, we should go."

"No way. Have you seen the bagels? Iggy here is having himself one of those bad boys."

Alex wasn't sure what to do. He stood next to Iggy in silence as the line gradually advanced.

After a few minutes, they reached the front. A short woman stood behind the counter, her hair gray and curly, her brown eyes sparkling with interest and intelligence.

"What can I get for you two young men?" she asked, flashing a warm smile.

A bagel with cream cheese and a coffee," Iggy said.

"And for you?" she said, turning to Alex, her infectious smile still firmly in place.

"Oh ... um ... a cappuccino and a croissant, please," Alex replied, grinning back despite his unease. For a moment he was reminded of his mom, for this woman, while older, radiated the same warmth and positivity.

"That will be sixteen dollars, please," she said. Iggy handed over the money and they stepped aside to let the next person order.

A young barista busied herself over an ancient-yet-pristine coffee machine, which spat and hissed as she warmed the milk, while a man handed them their croissant and bagel in a brown paper bag.

Moments later they emerged back into the dingy street, Iggy already biting into his bagel.

"Excuse me," said the older boy, not even bothering to look up as someone barred their way.

But Alex saw who it was instantly.

"Um ... hi," he said, swallowing nervously.

"And just what do you two think you're doing?" Captain Bailey asked, hands on hips and a look of fury on her face.

34 | Iggy Unrepentant

The drive back to Hope was not fun. Captain Bailey had remained stonily silent as she strode back to the pickup trucks where the others were already waiting. No one spoke as they got in the vehicles and drove out of town. But the instant they had left the main highway and taken the unsealed road into the forest, the harangue began.

"What the smeck were you thinking?" Captain Bailey started.

"I was thinking I wanted a bagel," Iggy replied nonchalantly.

"Against my express orders."

"You told me not to eat a bagel? Are you sure? I don't remember that."

"You know what I mean. I told you to get the musical equipment and come straight back."

"So what? I changed the plan. Big deal. We weren't caught, were we? Anyway, you should be thanking me after what happened at the music store. Alex-the-dexter-Franklin here almost got us caught by the Regs. Lucky I was on hand to save the day."

"What?" asked Captain Bailey and Locke together.

"Yeah, the Regs came in and *this* dexter confessed we were from Lincoln. But I saved us."

Iggy explained what had happened at Neil's Music Emporium while Alex sat silently, embarrassed at how Iggy described his actions but not sure how to defend himself. No one spoke as the vehicle labored up a steep hill, its engine straining, its wheels churning up dust.

"You're sure the Regulator said what happened at Lincoln High was a fire?" Locke asked at last.

"Yeah, I'm sure. And I'm sure he mentioned you by name, old man. He said it would be the electric chair for you," Iggy said, smirking.

"They have to catch me first, of course," Locke said quietly. "And then you went and got a bagel at …?"

"Fran's Fooderia," Alex chimed in, glad to move the conversation away from their embarrassing encounter with the Regs.

"Fran's place?" Locke said with interest. "And did you meet the eponymous owner?"

"The epo-what-now?" Iggy asked.

"Did you meet Fran? She would be in her mid-sixties, short, curly hair, smiles a lot."

"Don't think so, although there was an *uber* tidy woman when we came in," Iggy said, grinning lasciviously.

"Yes, we did meet Fran," Alex said, correcting him. "She served us at the counter, remember?"

Iggy frowned and shrugged.

"How did she seem?" Locke asked Alex eagerly. "Was she … alright?"

"Yes. She was very friendly … just as you described her. She seemed nice. I got a good vibe from her," Alex admitted.

"I'm glad to hear it," Locke said, visibly relieved.

"Why? Do you know her?" Alex asked curiously.

"Yes. Not well, I confess. And it was many years ago now. But we would all know who Francesca Delano is if not for the MeChip."

Francesca Delano. The name sounded vaguely familiar, but Alex couldn't place it.

"Why should we know her?"

"Because Francesca Delano is the candidate who was robbed of victory the night Bill Davison stole the election."

"You mean—"

"I mean Francesca Delano is the lawfully-elected President of the United States."

35 | President Nobody

Alex couldn't speak. It seemed incredible to him that he'd just met the woman who by rights should have been president. What would life have been like if the MeChip hadn't been used to steal the election, Alex wondered? But Iggy seemed less impressed.

"So what? That's ancient history now. She wasn't president in the end, was she? She must have been a loser to let them win like that," Iggy declared.

"She was not a loser," Locke replied firmly, an edge of irritation in his voice.

"Okay, okay, keep your hair on old man."

"Why is she in Fairview?" Alex asked.

"She retired there after losing the election," Locke replied.

"But why didn't she challenge the result?"

"Because she thought she'd genuinely lost. She was wearing a MeChip—still is, I imagine—and was fed the same lies as everyone else."

"And she didn't suspect anything?"

"I'm not sure, but I think not. If Francesca Delano has a flaw it is that she tends to see the positive in *everyone*. I don't think it would have occurred to her that she'd been cheated, especially in such a monstrous way."

"More fool her, then," Iggy announced.

"You could use some of her positivity yourself, young man," Locke said, glaring at Iggy.

"Look where it got her," Iggy shot back.

Locke was about to say more when Captain Bailey braked, easing the pickup to a halt. Looking through the windshield, Alex saw a barrier across the road. A moment later two of Bailey's troopers stepped from behind trees, laz-rifles cradled in their arms, their bodies camouflaged in olive-green fatigues. Captain Bailey wound down the window and gave the password. The soldiers saluted smartly, the barrier was raised and they drove on.

Five minutes later they were back in Hope. Now they had the equipment they needed, it was time to put the next phase of the plan into operation.

36 | Ode to Freedom

Abby's fingers ran deftly across the keys as the song began. Softly at first, it rose to a crescendo as Tom stormed the party with a crash of drums, Sol's bass throbbed urgently under the melody and Alex's X-shaped guitar soared majestically above, strident and strong. Finally, Alex's vocals cut through the heady mix with words uplifting and filled with hope and expectation, desire and dream-filled longing:

> *"Freedom for all in the land,*
> *Rise up in our rebellion,*
> *Let the flames of truth burn bright,*
> *To set us free for we are one,*
> *Never fear the great attempt,*
> *For in the end, we will prevail,*
> *Sisters, brothers, must unite*
> *Together we can never fail!"*

The song ended in a perfect maelstrom of music, drums smashing down one last time as the lead guitar faded out, its final note a mere echo, a hint of what had gone before, like the last drops of rain at the end of a thunderstorm.

Alex looked from Sol to Tom to Abby.

No one spoke. But Tom was already grinning, a huge smile spreading across his freckled face. Sol tilted his head to one side thoughtfully, then nodded.

"That was amazing!" screamed a voice through the speaker system. Alex looked up and saw Harriet smiling through the glass and giving them two thumbs up from the next room, where she was sitting at the mixing desk of their converted music studio. Behind her, Electa and Sybil grinned and cheered.

A moment later they had burst through the connecting door, smiling and clapping.

"Come on, bring it in!" Tom shouted enthusiastically as the seven of them came together in a spontaneous group hug, dancing and jumping on the spot for many millisecs before finally drawing apart.

"So ... it was good, then?" Alex asked at last.

"Good? Really, Alex? You dexter, it was brilliant!" Sybil gushed, as Electa nodded beside her.

"What do you think, Abby?" Alex asked, looking at her and feeling his face turn hot.

She didn't answer at first but looked at him thoughtfully, biting her lower lip and shaking her head.

"Not good?" he asked anxiously as the silence dragged on.

"Alex, if you don't know by now that you're a great musician, then I really can't help you!" she said teasingly. "Someone needs to persuade him he's got talent. And that goes for you guys, too," she said, turning to Sol and Tom. "You were brilliant!"

"Hey, you were pretty smeckin' awesome yourself," Tom said, smiling back.

"No kidding!" Sybil cooed.

"Locke's gonna love it!" Harriet agreed.

"And it sounds like his work is coming along quickly, too. They just have to complete one more task before we can broadcast," Electa informed them.

Alex licked his lips nervously. Broadcasting already? It seemed like only yesterday since they'd come back from Fairview with the gear they'd needed. In fact, it had been three weeks of preparations and non-stop practice. They'd been so busy it had passed in a blur.

"I'm gonna celebrate with some lunch. Anyone care to join me?" Tom asked.

The others all nodded but Alex shook his head. "I'll catch you up. I just need to check on something."

As the rest of them filed out, Abby cast an inquiring glance back at Alex, who was now pretending to scrutinize his microphone. He waited a minute until they'd all gone before finally stepping out of the small studio. Instead of making his way down the path back into town, however, he walked towards a second building that also sat perched on top of the small hill overlooking Hope.

One of the town's soldiers was stationed at the front door but she nodded at Alex in recognition and stepped aside to let him enter. Inside, several townsfolk were busy on old computers and other pieces of antiquated technology, too immersed in their work to notice the young man in their midst. A moment later he was in a short corridor, its ceiling light blinking on and off as if the bulb needed replacing. He stopped at the last door, paused, then knocked.

"Come in."

He took a deep breath, pushed the door open, and walked inside.

37 | The Breakthrough

"I was wondering when you'd visit," said the man behind the desk, his piercing green eyes fixed on Alex.

Dr. Locke closed his laptop and motioned for Alex to sit down. The teenager looked across the desk at his old mentor. As he stared into the man's eyes, he felt a mix of resentment and sympathy. He was still angry with Locke for keeping so much of the truth hidden. Things between them had been strained ever since that night they'd argued over the campfire. And Alex had been so busy recently that he just hadn't had time to track Locke down and speak with him in private. Judging by the dark smudges under his eyes and the new lines that had multiplied across his forehead, Locke had been working hard, too. Still, Alex hadn't forgotten Locke's promise to tell him the truth once they reached Hope. And now, before anything else happened, he was determined to get it.

"I'm here for answers," Alex said at last, not quite sure how to begin.

"Of course you are. And I intend to give them to you," Locke replied calmly.

"You do?"

"Yes—if I can. A promise is a promise, after all," Locke said, his eyes fixed on Alex's as his lips curled into a smile.

"Oh ... well ..." Alex began uncertainly. He'd expected it to be harder than this and, now the time had come, found he wasn't sure where to start.

"Can I ask you just one question first?" Locke said.

"Sure."

"How are rehearsals going?" he asked, leaning forward in his chair and resting his elbows on the desk.

"Well. Really well. Everyone seems to think we've nailed it."

"And you're happy with the song choice?"

"Oh yeah. I mean, we didn't really know much about this Beethoven guy until you suggested him. It was a bit hard at first to figure out how to turn his music into something a rock band would play. But we managed it in the end."

"Good. I'm glad you like the 'Beethoven guy,'" Locke said with a smile. "And the lyrics?"

"We changed them a bit. For instance, we altered 'Ode to Joy' to 'Ode to Freedom' and made it a bit more—I don't know—modern, I guess. But everyone seems to like them."

"I can see why. Abby showed them to me the other day and I thought they were excellent. True to the original spirit of the words but more up-to-date."

"Thanks."

Alex was about to speak again when there was a knock on the door—a succession of quick, urgent raps that made the flimsy plywood shake. Before Locke could respond the handle turned and a man rushed in. He was tall with long, black hair and round glasses that magnified his eyes to an almost alarming degree. He was beaming so broadly that Alex wondered how he could hold the smile without it hurting. But he seemed joyful rather than pained as he addressed Locke.

"We've done it. We're in the mainframe!" he declared jubilantly.

"Excellent," Locke replied, eyes shining. "And no tracers?"

"Not a sign."

"Not even with their recent AI-assisted enhancements?"

"Completely undetected. Do you want to come look?"

"In a little while. I'm chatting with Alex right now."

The man looked at Alex, opening his gigantic eyes even wider in surprise as he registered the teenager's presence for the first time.

"Don't be too long, John. The team's eager to show you." He turned and retreated from the room, leaving the door wide open as the echo of his footsteps retreated down the corridor. Sighing, John Locke stood up, walked around the desk and closed the door, then sat down again.

"Professor Chang has a brilliant brain—indeed, we are fortunate he found his way to Hope last year—but he can be a little absent-minded at times," Locke said, still smiling.

"It sounds like good news, though," Alex observed.

"Very good news, Alex. It means we are almost ready."

"How soon do you think we'll be able to perform?"

"With Professor Chang's breakthrough, I'd say the day after tomorrow."

"Oh ... wow ... not in a week or two?" Alex asked, swallowing.

"No. This brings everything forward. Nervous?" Locke asked, looking at Alex carefully.

"A little."

"Good. A few butterflies in the stomach aren't a bad thing. They keep you sharp. But you will be brilliant. I know it.

"Couldn't we just, you know, record the song first, then upload it and play it to everyone later?" Alex asked hopefully. "It would mean less pressure on us to get our performance just right."

"I did think of that," Locke replied, scratching his chin. "But the recording equipment we have here isn't up to the standard we would need. Besides, there is nothing more powerful, in my view, than a live performance. You must keep in mind that we're trying to produce a music so moving and impressive it can defeat the MeChip. In that regard, a live show is most likely to deliver what we need."

"But now it's time for your questions, Alex," Locke continued. "What would you like to know?" he asked, pressing his fingertips together and waiting expectantly

38 | Locke Opens Up

"So ... so you still think music is the best way to beat the MeChip?" Alex asked nervously as an image came unbidden into his brain of him freezing at the critical moment.

"What other choice do we have?" Locke replied, eyebrows raised.

"I was thinking about what you showed me at the safe house back in Lincoln. You remember ... you helped me fight off the MeChip's control and see the vase of flowers for what it was. I even transformed it into an owl. And then, later on that day, I was able to break General Arnold's control when I met him by the train tracks. Abby did, too, at least for a millisec."

"I remember," Locke said, eyes narrowing. "You're asking if there is a way to defeat the MeChip through strength of mind? And I have thought more about it. You both showed remarkable mental fortitude in overcoming the MeChip's influence. And the fact you could change what you saw in our little experiment with the flowers certainly made me wonder ..." he said, trailing off abstractedly and staring out of the window, his eyes unfocused.

"Wonder what?" Alex asked curiously.

"Well, if you could change how your own MeChip works, could you control the MeChips of others?"

"Is that possible?"

"Perhaps. MeChips can communicate with each other, of course, to send texts and make calls, and so on. The closer they are physically, the stronger the link. But—"

"But what?"

"I'm still not sure how we use that skill to defeat every MeChip in the land. Even if it was possible it would probably operate like that remote control I built—influencing a handful of people close by. No, our current plan to use music is the only one I can think of that could work at the scale we need and liberate every American all at once."

"Alright," Alex said at last. So he would have to play after all. Live. To every single person in the country. He swallowed again and looked away.

"If it's any consolation, I believe fully and completely in you," Locke said, as if reading Alex's mind. "There's really nothing to fear. Keep rehearsing and, when the time comes, you'll know the music so well you'll find it almost plays itself," he said, smiling. "But back to the questions you had. What else did you wish to know?"

"I wanted to ask about my family."

"Your mother?"

"Actually, my dad. My *real* dad, I mean."

"But of course. Have you asked your mother about him?"

"Um ... no," Alex admitted.

"Perhaps you should, Alex. More of her memories of him might be coming back."

"I would, but she's always with *him* ... with ... you know, the man we're all calling *Ben*," he said resentfully.

"And you've been avoiding them?" Locke guessed shrewdly.

"No ... well, yes. But I *have* been kinda busy," Alex replied, trying to justify himself.

"I understand. It must feel awkward, to say the least, to see your mother with this man."

"That's an understatement. I don't know what to say to him and he's always with her."

"I sympathize, Alex. It's a horrible situation. Try to keep in mind, though, that this man you look on as a stranger acted as your father for five years. And he, too, was deceived by the MeChip, just as you and your mother were. He acted in good faith, truly believing himself to be your parent. May I ask, was he kind to you during that time?"

"Yeah, he was," Alex admitted.

"That is something, at least. Remember—he is as much the MeChip's victim as anyone else. He, too, deserves your compassion and understanding."

"I get it. But I don't think I can deal with that. Not yet, anyways," Alex said, looking at the carpet.

"Which is entirely natural. These things take time, Alex. They will understand. What other questions do you have for me?"

"I wanted to know about the boy. You know, the one the Fixers brought to replace me that night you showed up at my house."

"Ah, yes. Him."

"You said he would be my replacement but I never saw him again. I mean, he wasn't with my parents when General Arnold brought them to the school for the Best Band contest."

"No."

"So what happened?"

"I'm not sure. I suspect Arnold changed his plans when you escaped that night. Perhaps he considered it too risky to have your replacement installed when you were still at large. Imagine if both of you had shown up at school."

"So where is the other boy now?"

"I wish I knew. My guess is they placed him with another family. In all likelihood, his real parents died and they were looking to pair him with a new family. Probably that will still happen, or already has. It will just be someplace else now."

"So he was a bit like me, then?"

"What do you mean?"

"Well, his parents must be dead. And my dad is, too ... isn't he?" asked Alex, hoping against hope that Locke would contradict him, tell him it wasn't true. But Locke didn't even try.

"Yes, Alex, your father is almost certainly no longer alive. I'm sorry."

"You said *almost* certainly. Could something else have happened?"

"Most people are taken away by the Fixers because they've died from pollution or disease," he said, speaking slowly as if choosing his words carefully. "But sometimes—very rarely—they may be taken away for other reasons."

"Like what?"

"Well, if someone shows signs of breaking the MeChip's programming, for instance."

"And what happens then?" Alex asked excitedly.

"Nothing good, I'm afraid. If the Fixers realize what's going on they may replace that person and bring them to laboratories for testing and ... um ... fixing."

"What does that mean?"

"Sometimes they will operate on the person's brain, cutting out the part that shows free will."

"And does that work?"

"In a way. That person will survive but be much less intelligent, a shadow of their former self and easy prey for the MeChip. Most of the time, however, they consider an operation to be too much of an effort, and will simply murder the person instead."

"Has anyone ever escaped the MeChip's control and *not* been caught?"

"Maggie Corbin—the woman we met in the woods and who lived in the tower—seems to have become free of the MeChip's grasp, although her memories of what occurred were unclear."

"Alright. Anyone else?"

"Possibly. I suspect it happens only rarely, though."

"But didn't you tell me one time that MeChips can't read your thoughts?" Alex asked, seizing on an idea.

"That is correct. While the MeChip can understand a range of simple mental instructions so users can make calls or watch their favorite show, for instance, they are not mind readers."

"So people might get free of its programming all the time and the Fixers wouldn't know?" Alex suggested.

"No, Alex. The MeChip has many ways to monitor you. Its controllers would almost certainly find out if you were breaking its control.

"How?"

"For a start, MeChips contain a self-sensor that alerts the Fixers and their allies in case of a malfunction."

"But what if it's not malfunctioning? What if somehow a person just starts to break free of the control mechanism but the MeChip is still technically working just fine? That way, the controllers wouldn't think anything was wrong, would they?"

"Perhaps not. But the MeChip also contains an audio component; it can literally hear and record anything you say."

"Why does that matter?"

"It means if you started to suspect your MeChip was controlling you and you confided in someone—in *anyone*—then the Fixers would find out."

"But ... but there's still a chance my father broke the MeChip's control and escaped, no? I mean even with all of the safeguards you mentioned, it's still technically possible," Alex persisted, unwilling to give up on the idea his dad might still be alive.

"It is possible in theory," Locke admitted. "But do not forget what your mother said a few weeks ago over the campfire; she told us she had a memory of your father getting sick and dying."

"But what if she was wrong? She did say the memory was hazy."

"Alex, the chances of her returning memories misleading her are so remote I do not think we can give them any credence. Hard as it is to accept, I cannot see how he might have survived, Alex. I'm sorry."

They sat in silence for a moment as Alex absorbed what he'd just heard. It seemed almost impossible, based on what Locke had just told him, that his father had somehow escape and was still alive somewhere. And the idea that his dad had been captured and operated on was too horrible to contemplate. Compared with that, Alex thought bleakly, it was probably better if his father *had* died. With an effort, he pushed that thought aside as a new idea struck him.

"That brain operation you mentioned. Is that what they were going to do to me the night you came to our home? Replace me with the other boy and then operate on my brain?"

"Again, I cannot say for certain. But if I had to guess then I would say yes. They had clearly concluded you were too much of a risk to them to leave you alone."

There was a further silence as Alex contemplated how close he'd come to this horrible fate.

"What else can I tell you?" Locke prompted him after a few seconds of silence.

"Oh, right. Well, what about Iggy?"

"What about him?"

"Don't you think there's something weird going on with him?"

"What do you mean?"

"For one, something felt really off when the two of us confronted General Arnold down by the train tracks."

"Can you explain?"

"Arnold didn't try hard enough to stop us. He didn't even reach for his gun or chase after us when we ran. Which makes no sense. Why would he let us escape?"

"I have a theory, but it's nothing more than that," Locke said at last. "I could be wrong and without knowing more of the facts—"

"You're going to say you can't tell me, aren't you?"

"I'm going to tell you I'd rather not speculate. And I think I need to speak with Iggy first."

"That won't be easy. He doesn't like you."

"I know," said Locke, grimacing. "Whatever General Arnold told him about me seems to have struck a chord for some reason."

"Is that why you chose me instead of him for your plan?"

"That is a very simple question with a very complicated answer. There are a lot of reasons I want you to play when we try to break the MeChip's power. It would take a long time to explain them all. But I can tell you categorically it has nothing to do with Iggy Elgar or General Arnold. In fact, the main reason I chose you is because you are a very gifted musician."

Alex waited for Locke to continue but it appeared he had said all he planned to on that topic. He sat looking at Alex expectantly. Reluctantly, Alex moved on to another issue that had been bothering him—perhaps the most important issue of all.

"You said there was a connection between my father being taken away five years ago and your plans for the MeChip. Can you tell me what it is?"

"I'm glad you asked that, Alex, for it is critical to what is happening. It's also very personal, so I hope you'll indulge me by letting me tell you a little more about my story ... my history, if you like. Because this is, in part, a story about family."

"Okay ..." said Alex, not sure where this was going.

"You may recall me telling you when we were at my safe house that I moved to Lincoln after being ousted from Happy Corps by General Arnold. Do you remember the reason I gave you?"

"Um ... was it something to do with a family connection?" Alex said uncertainly.

"That is correct. But there is more to it than that. My link with the town is not through some distant cousin or elderly aunt. In fact, I grew up in Lincoln. Much like you, Alex, I was born and raised there, had friends and family, went to Lincoln High, and even had a high-school sweetheart—hard as that may be to believe when you look at me now," he said, his eyes twinkling. "But it's all true. I lived there for 18 years until leaving for college in California, and returned many times after that for holidays and vacations."

"So you knew the town when you were a kid. Why does that matter?" Alex asked, frowning.

"It matters, Alex, because of whom I knew back then. The children I grew up with, the folks I got to know in Lincoln then and later on, and what happened to these people as they grew up."

"What do you mean?" Alex asked, his curiosity growing.

"Perhaps I should start with a family I became close to after college. They were originally from England. The father was an engineer hired by Bright Green Mining." Locke began. "They arrived—"

But he never finished his sentence for at that moment the door burst open and Sybil rushed in.

"Dr. Locke—John—I really need to talk to you and ... oh," she said, pausing as she saw Alex.

He could tell at once she'd been crying. Her eyes were red-rimmed and still glistening. Blushing, she put a hand up to her face.

"Are you alright, Sybil?" Locke asked, standing up and looking at her with concern.

"Yes ... no," she replied, her voice trembling. "You said to come see you if we had any memories of the past or needed your help, and something's happened. But if this isn't a good time ..." She trailed off, looking from Locke to Alex.

There was an awkward silence as Alex tried to decide how to respond. He wasn't done—not even half-done—with Locke. He still had many questions and had a feeling Locke was about to tell him something of the greatest importance. But on the other hand, Sybil seemed in a bad way and in urgent need of Locke's help, too.

"It's okay, I can go," Alex said after a pause. "I should probably grab some lunch before the cafeteria closes anyway. Can we—"

"Continue this conversation later?" John Locke said. "Yes, of course. Come back soon and we'll talk more. Agreed?"

"Definitely," Alex replied, holding Locke's gaze. In that moment something passed between them. He wasn't sure what, exactly, but somehow he felt strangely lighter, less weighed down with responsibility; as if the trust he'd had in his mentor before their argument in the forest had not been lost as he'd feared, merely misplaced for a little while. He cast one last look at Locke, aimed what he hoped was a reassuring smile at Sybil and left, closing the door firmly behind him.

39 | Tom's Cunning Plan

Alex had just started walking down the hill to the cafeteria when someone came rushing out of the music studio, colliding with him and sending him staggering backwards.

"Sorry! Are you okay?" said Electa, looking as surprised as Alex was.

"I'm fine. No harm done," Alex replied. "But what are you doing here? I thought you were having lunch with the others?"

"Oh, I forgot ... um ... this," she said, holding up her satchel.

"Are *you* okay?" Alex asked, noticing Electa's distracted expression.

"Me? Yeah, I'm fine. Just peachy. And how about you? Excited to perform to the whole country?"

"Oh, that. Yeah, I guess."

"You don't sound it. Nervous?"

"It's giving me the jeepsters just thinking about it," Alex confessed.

"I'm not surprised. I mean, it's a big deal. Still, rehearsals are going great. You sound fantastic!" she said, patting his arm reassuringly.

"Thanks."

They walked in silence down the hill, both apparently lost in thought.

"Here's the cafeteria. I'd better get back to school. See ya!" Electa waved over her shoulder as she strode away, leaving Alex to enter the food hall alone.

As he walked through the entrance he almost bumped into someone else.

"Hey, why don't you watch where you're … oh, it's you," said Leah Mecon, her frown instantly transforming into a smile. "How's the music going?"

"Pretty well, actually. You should ask Electa. She just heard our last rehearsal."

"Great idea. I'm heading to school right now. Before I go, though, care to tell me any more about your mystery feud with Iggy?" she said, raising an eyebrow.

"There's not much to tell. We just don't like each other, is all."

"That's what he says. But why do I have a feeling you're both holding back?" she asked, tilting her head and eyeing him appraisingly.

Alex shrugged and smiled apologetically. He really didn't want to get into this right now but he didn't want to seem rude, either.

"Alright, keep your secrets then—both of you. But I'll find out in the end," she said, tapping her nose and smiling as she departed.

The next two days were hectic: hours spent in final rehearsals, the last-minute checking of gear, and hooking their instruments up to all the equipment Locke and his team had engineered; then endless soundchecks and tests and yet more tests to make sure everything was in perfect working order. Alex was so busy he barely had time to think about what he'd learned from Locke, let alone figure out when he might speak with his mentor again, grab a moment with Abby, or even check in with his mom.

As the day of the performance dawned, the thought that he would be performing live to the entire country that evening kept upsetting his equilibrium, sending his heart racing and his mind swirling, like a leaf tossed and blown every which way by a wild autumn wind. Trying to outrun the fear, he flung himself still harder into work, jumping in to help with every task and chore required.

By mid-afternoon, they were done. No more soundchecks were needed, no more rehearsals, no final fittings for the glammed-up Revolutionary War era costumes Locke had insisted they wear. The old man had nodded, satisfied with everything, and told them to relax for a few hours and take things easy before the big night. Disappointed there was nothing left to distract his brain, Alex had plodded down the hill with Tom and Sol.

He decided to take a shower, walking over to the communal bathrooms and hoping the warm water would relax him. It didn't. He entered the cabin feeling tense and more nervous than he'd thought possible. When he saw Tom, however, he knew he wasn't the only one with something on his mind.

His friend was sitting on the couch, tapping his knees with his hands and nodding his head, as if to a beat Alex couldn't hear. He was biting his lip and appeared preoccupied, distracted.

"Do you have the jeepsters, too?"

Tom looked up at him and started, as if he hadn't even noticed his friend enter the building.

"What's that, Alex?"

"I said are you nervous? About the performance?"

"That? Oh, no. I never get nervous about playing music. You know that," Tom replied.

"Then what's up? You seem ... I don't know ... agitated."

Tom stared at the ground, bit his lip again, then finally looked back up at Alex.

"I've been thinking about something and I've just come to a decision," Tom said at last.

"What is it?"

"I've decided to tell Sybil I like her. A lot."

"Oh, right."

"So? What do you think?" Tom asked, looking at Alex expectantly.

"It sounds fine. But are you sure? I thought you liked Leah and Electa as well?"

"No, Alex. What are you talking about? I said they were tidy and they are. But I've always liked Sybil. You know that," he answered decisively, frowning at his friend.

Was this true, Alex wondered? Thinking back, Tom *had* seemed keen on her for a long time. Then again, he'd also appeared keen on any number of other girls, too.

"Now she's heard us rehearsing and seen how smeckin' awesome I am on drums, it's the perfect time to tell her how I feel," Tom continued, not noticing Alex's uncertainty.

"Are you sure?" Alex asked again.

"Yes, I'm sure. And I'm sure she likes me, too. Think about it. She's been helping out with our rehearsals for days now. She keeps saying how stellar we are. She even said my drumming was good, remember? So she must be interested, right?" Tom asked, looking to Alex for confirmation.

Alex thought back over the last few days. Harriet, Electa, and Sybil had been there a lot, it was true. Perhaps Tom was correct. But could he be sure? And was the timing right? Sybil had seemed miserable when she'd gate-crashed Locke's office the other day. Would she want someone asking her out right now? Alex didn't want Tom getting turned down by a girl *again*.

"Where's Sol?" Alex asked after a millisec, wondering what he'd say about this.

"Gone out. With Harriet, I think. Something about a bass guitar," Tom said distractedly. "But let's stay focused on the important thing here—me," he continued. "I have a plan and you're going to help me, okay?"

"Maybe. Let's hear it first."

"It's really simple. You and I go over to Sybil's cabin. If any of her roommates are there you tell them you need to talk to them about something outside."

"Harriet won't be there," Alex said. "You just told me she's with Sol."

"Oh, yeah. Right. So it could only be Abby. If she's there, you make some excuse and get her to leave the cabin. Then I let Sybil know the good news about how I feel," Tom declared, grinning.

"And you're sure you want to do this?"

"Yes, I'm sure, Alex. Why do you keep asking? I've thought it all through. And you'll be my wingman. What could possibly go wrong?"

"Alright," Alex agreed reluctantly.

"Great! Let's go."

They left the cabin and made their way across a clearing and towards another row of wooden buildings, Tom leading the way and almost skipping with excitement. "Oh man, I can't wait to see the look on her face. Now remember, if Abby's there, you get her to come outside with you. Okay?"

"Okay, Tom," Alex sighed.

They reached the door to one of the cabins. Tom took a deep breath, reached for the handle and, without knocking, bounded confidently inside as Alex followed a couple of steps behind.

Tom had been right. Sybil was there. And she wasn't alone. But it wasn't Abby with her, or even Harriet.

It was Electa. She was sitting with Sybil on one of the beds.

And the two of them were kissing.

40 | Sybil's Secret

For several seconds, the two girls didn't notice the intruders. Then Sybil opened her eyes for a millisec, caught sight of them, and leaped up, pulling away from Electa and staring in confusion at Alex and Tom.

"What the ... what's wrong? Oh ..." Electa said, turning around and seeing them, too.

"What's happening?" Tom asked, blinking rapidly as if trying to clear his vision, unable to comprehend what he was seeing.

"I would have thought that was pretty obvious," Electa said calmly.

"But girls don't date other girls. I've never ... this never—"

"Only chipslaves talk that way," Electa cut in.

"What?" Tom said, still looking bewildered.

"She means it's the MeChip that makes girls only date boys," Sybil said, speaking at last. She was talking quickly and sounded out of breath, as if she'd been running a marathon. Her face was red, perhaps even redder than her hair.

Tom just gaped at her unable to speak, so Sybil carried on, her words rapid and staccato, like a machine gun spitting out bullets: "Ever since my MeChip stopped working I've started to have different feelings about things and I didn't know what was going on exactly and was feeling guilty about it all but Electa told me it was okay for girls to like other girls and boys to like other boys and it was just our MeChips controlling us. And then I spoke with John—with Dr. Locke—and he told me it was all true. And he told me to be true to myself and so that's what I'm doing," she ended, her tone defiant, as if daring Alex and Tom to contradict her.

"But I thought maybe ... I thought perhaps you liked—"

"Liked you, Tom?" Sybil asked, cutting him off. "I thought so, too. But that was back in Lincoln when the MeChip was still switched on, still controlling me. Now I know different. I mean, I do like you, Tom, really. Just as a friend, is all."

There was a long silence as the two teenagers stared at each other.

"Well, good luck," Tom said finally, turning around and leaving as abruptly as he'd arrived.

Alex glanced at Sybil and Electa and shrugged. "I'd better go, too. Sorry."

He caught up with Tom in the clearing a millisec later.

"Are you okay?"

"Okay? No. I'm not okay at all. I guess I ... it's just that ..." he trailed off, unable to finish his sentence.

"Can I do anything to help?"

"Later, maybe. Right now I just need to be alone. I think I'm gonna take a walk, clear my head." And with that Tom took off, striding towards the nearest trees without waiting for an answer. A moment later and he was lost from view, his lanky frame swallowed by the forest as he left Alex alone in the clearing.

"What's with Tom?" came a voice from behind him.

Alex spun around, half-wishing he could have some time alone, too, to process what had just happened.

Then he saw who it was and changed his mind.

"Listen, I think we need to talk," he said, his eyes fixed on hers.

"Okay," she said. "A walk?"

He nodded and they fell into step together, taking a path in the opposite direction to Tom as they headed out of town.

41 | The Clouds Part

"So what *was* up with Tom?" Abby asked again as she and Alex followed one of the trails leading out of Hope.

"We just saw Sybil with someone else. I think they're dating."

"I see. And Tom kinda likes Sybil, right?"

Alex nodded.

"So who was Sybil with? No, let me guess … Electa?"

"How did you—?"

"Intuition, I guess. And using my eyes and ears," she said, smiling.

"But that's not something that happens—"

"In Lincoln? I know. But things are different here. The MeChip's not controlling us anymore. People's real memories—and real feelings—are being set free."

"That's kinda what I wanted to talk with you about," Alex said, seizing the moment. "I was wondering if you'd had any more memories of your past life?"

"Anything in particular?"

"Well … you know … memories of us," Alex said, feeling self-conscious. He snatched a glance at her and saw she was smiling.

"I know what you mean, Alex. I'm just pranking you. And yes, I remember more stuff every day."

"Like what?"

"I remember going back to the treehouse with you. And I remember talking with my friends about you and them being sure you liked me."

"Oh right," Alex replied, reddening. "But what about him—Iggy, I mean. What do you remember about that … um … situation?"

"That's the weird part, Alex. The more time passes, the less my memories of dating Iggy seem real. It's almost as if—"

"As if the MeChip put them there?"

"I think so," Abby admitted at last.

"I don't want to say I told you so," Alex said.

"Then don't," she said in a tone Alex couldn't read at all. Was she annoyed or was she pranking him again?

"Have you spoken with Iggy about any of this?" he asked at last.

"No. I'm not sure if he's been avoiding me or if it's just that I've been so busy, but I've hardly seen him these past few weeks."

They walked in silence as the trail led them deeper into the forest. Occasionally there came the sound of a bird call or the rustle of an unknown animal among the bushes. The wind whispered in the topmost leaves and from time to time Alex caught sight of a cloud-filled sky.

"I wonder if he's started to remember things, too?" Alex said. "Maybe that's why he's avoiding you. I bet he knows you weren't really dating after all."

"Maybe. But what about you, Alex?"

"What about me?"

"You've known the truth for longer; had more time to think about it. How are you feeling?"

"How am I feeling?"

"Yes, Alex. How are you feeling about all of this ... about me?" she asked, stopping and turning to face him, her eyes locked on his.

"I'm hoping you remember everything as it really is, remember once and for all that you were never really dating Iggy and that you and I were going to talk about the future with no distractions."

"And you haven't been distracted by anything yourself lately? Or anyone?" she said, raising an eyebrow and folding her arms across her chest.

"What do you mean?"

"I mean a certain trainee doctor by the name of Leah Mecon."

"Oh. What about Leah?" Alex said, looking away.

"She seems interested in you, don't you think?"

"Um, no … I don't think so."

"Are you sure, Alex? You're not the sharpest tool in the shed when it comes to relationships, you know."

Alex was about to reply when Abby held up a hand for silence and looked around, scanning the trees.

"Did you hear that?" she whispered, still looking left and right.

Alex paused, straining to hear something, anything. He was about to suggest she'd been imagining it when he, too, heard a noise. It was coming from off to their left.

"Let's investigate. Don't make a sound," she whispered, her mouth close to his ear.

The two of them crept quietly forward, stopping every few seconds to listen. There was no doubt at all something was out there. They advanced cautiously, edging forward until Alex finally figured out what it was.

Voices. They were definitely human voices. Exchanging another glance with Abby, they stole slowly forward until they reached the edge of a small clearing.

Two figures were standing in the center, two figures Alex would have recognized anywhere. They were talking and smiling. The shorter one had copper-colored hair while the taller one was blond. He whispered something and she laughed, then leaned forward to kiss him. Suddenly, the clouds broke apart and the sun burst through, illuminating the two figures like actors lit up on a stage.

Alex watched them for several millisecs, feeling strangely surprised but also as if he'd somehow expected this all along. The two people seemed blissfully unaware they were being observed as they continue to kiss in the bright sunshine.

Alex felt a hand on his arm and turned to see Abby motioning for them to retreat. Together, they quietly retraced their steps, emerging onto the trail and making their way back in the direction of Hope. It was only when they'd put a few hundred yards between themselves and the other couple that they stopped and turned to look at each other once more.

"I guess that puts paid to my theory Leah Mecon likes you," Abby said, biting her lip and smiling.

"I guess so, since she definitely wasn't faking that kiss with Iggy."

42 | Abby Interrupted

"**I**nteresting. Definitely interesting," Alex observed, trying to sound casual.

"Is that how you'd describe what we just saw?" Abby asked, tilting her head to one side as she looked at him.

"Yeah. I mean your theory about Leah liking me was way wrong, and Iggy's obviously realized you two aren't dating, unless ..."

"Unless what?"

"Unless he's two-timing you," Alex said, trying to keep a straight face.

"As if!" Abby said, arms crossed.

"Either way, Iggy and Leah are an item now, which is, like I say, interesting," he added, smiling at last.

"Interesting for whom? Them?"

"Of course for them. But for others too."

"Who else?"

"I don't know. You maybe?"

"Maybe," she said teasingly, smiling too.

"And me, of course," he confessed.

"Oh, definitely you!" she laughed.

"Okay, I admit it," he said, holding up his hands in mock surrender. "But seriously, you know what this means?"

"Why don't you tell me, Alex?"

"It means you don't have a boyfriend, right?"

"Right," she nodded. "And since Leah's into Iggy, you don't have a wannabe girlfriend waiting in the wings either," she said, winking at him and taking a step closer.

"Nope. I'm free as a bird," he grinned.

"Then why don't we—"

"Alex! Abby! There you are," came a voice from nearby.

The two of them spun around just as Alex's mom emerged from a bend in the trail. Next to her was the man now known as Ben. They were holding hands.

"We were wondering where you'd got to," said Ben, looking from one to the other.

"Why?" Alex asked, trying to keep the edge of irritation out of his voice.

"John wants to see you both," his mom said.

"Dr. Locke's looking for us?" Alex asked, surprised.

"Yes. Can you head up to his office, please?"

"Sure," Abby and Alex said together.

"Oh, and guys, if I don't see you before the performance, good luck. I know you'll be absolutely wonderful," Alex's mom said, hugging Abby before taking her son in a fond embrace.

"Good luck, both of you," Ben added, patting Abby on the shoulder before offering his hand to Alex.

For a millisec Alex was tempted to ignore it or push it away. Then Locke's words came back to him. This man—whoever he really was—was as much a victim of the MeChip's lies as he was. And he'd acted in good faith as his father for five years. Sighing inwardly, Alex took the man's hand and shook it. "Thanks, Ben," he said, holding his gaze.

"Come on, Alex, we'd better go," Abby said quietly.

As they turned the corner in the path, Alex cast a quick look over his shoulder and caught a final glimpse of his mom and Ben. They were still holding hands as they watched the two teenagers head back into town.

43 | The Countdown

"So, where were we?" Abby said as the trail took another turn and the town of Hope appeared before them.

"I think we were about to talk about us," Alex said, his grin returning.

"Guys! There you are. Come on, Dr. L's looking for us." It was Tom. He'd emerged from behind one of the cabins and spotted them on the trail. Instantly, he began hurrying over.

"Seriously, what does someone have to do to get a little privacy around here?" Alex whispered as Tom approached.

"No idea. We're obviously cursed," Abby laughed, shaking her head in disbelief.

"To be continued?" Alex asked.

"Definitely."

"So are you coming? I think we're late," Tom said, now standing in front of them.

"Of course," Abby replied.

They started together through the town, past the school and the hospital and the cafeteria, before making their way up the steep path leading to the studio and Locke's office.

"You okay?" Alex asked Tom quietly as they labored up the hill together.

"I've been better. Seeing Sybil and Electa together was a shock. But I'll survive. I have to. Anyways, it's time to focus on the performance. We've got an entire country to impress," he said, managing to muster a half-smile.

"That's the spirit," Alex said, putting an arm around his friend's shoulders.

A few moments later and they had crested the hill. They passed Captain Bailey's troops, now numbering more than a dozen as they guarded the studio and the building Locke and his team were using. Millisecs later and they were in his office.

Sol was already there, sitting across the table from Locke who was chatting with him quietly.

"And now we're all here," he said looking at each of them in turn.

"You wanted to check something with us?" Tom asked.

"Actually, I wanted to check *in* with you all," Locke replied. "You are performing in just over an hour. How are you feeling?"

There was a short silence before anyone spoke.

"I don't know about the others, but I'm feeling pretty good, John," Abby said, glancing quickly at Alex before looking back at Locke.

"Good, good. And you, Tom? How are you feeling about the performance?"

"About the gig? Oh, I always feel good about playing drums," Tom replied, not quite sounding like his usual, exuberant self, but with a look of determination that told Alex he'd be just fine.

"And you, Sol?"

"Something you guys may not know about me is that I tend to worry about what might go wrong—," Sol said slowly.

"Oh, we know *that*," Tom said sarcastically.

"But I don't think we've ever been more ready to perform than we are right now," Sol added. "We couldn't be better prepared," he concluded.

"Coming from someone as thoughtful as you, Sol, that is praise indeed," John Locke said, nodding at him approvingly. "And how about you, Alex?" Locke said, turning to his protégé at last.

"I've got the jeepsters, I won't lie," Alex admitted. "But Sol's right; we've prepared for this moment so thoroughly I don't see what more we could have done."

"Excellent. And may I say how proud I am of you all," Locke declared, again looking at each of them in turn. "For your dedication, your focus, your commitment, and your bravery these past few weeks. Not to mention your prodigious musical talents," he added.

There was a silence as the five of them looked at each other, their eyes showing their mutual pride, respect and belief.

"So what are we waiting for?" Tom asked at last. "Let's go make history."

An hour later and they were in the studio ready to perform. Alex's X-guitar was strapped across his shoulders, a microphone close to his lips. On his left was Abby, her fingers poised over the keyboard, while on his right stood Sol, the bass guitar slung low over his torso. Behind him sat Tom, drumsticks in hand, while on the other side of the glass sitting in the sound booth was Harriet, who was running the mixing desk, and Locke, who was operating the equipment that would transmit their music to the entire nation. Behind them, three technicians were working the cameras, lights, and other gear.

Alex took a deep breath. He couldn't deny it; he had the jeepsters big time. Still, they weren't as bad as he'd expected. He thought back to their performance at Lincoln High a little over a month ago, the night they'd freed 1000 people from their MeChips. He'd been nervous then, too—so nervous he thought he might freeze again. But he hadn't. He'd done it then, wowing the crowd with his music. And he knew in his heart he could do it this time, too. In a way, this felt easier. After all, he wouldn't see all the people he was performing to. If he just focused on the studio and his playing, he felt sure it would be okay.

As Locke spoke into their earphones to let them know the five-minute countdown to transmission had begun, Alex felt more confident, and more prepared, than he ever had before. Honestly, he didn't see what could possibly stop them.

44 | Blast from the Past

The first sign anything was amiss was a single flicker of the lights. Was it just his imagination? Alex looked through the glass at Harriet and Locke to see if they'd noticed it, too. It was obvious from their expressions they had. Harriet was biting her lip and looking at the lamp on the desk, while Locke was frowning and motionless, tension etched in every line of his face.

The lights flickered again and then, a millisec later, came a sound like nothing Alex had heard before:

Whump! Boom! Whump!

It shook the building as one blast followed another, deep and dreadful, deafening and deadening, sending shockwaves of sound racing through Alex's body, like an earthquake and the crash of thunder and the scream of a tsunami all rolled into one. Alex struggled to stay on his feet as the second blast struck, then the third. His head felt like it might explode from the noise, the vibrations, and he clutched his ears and closed his eyes as the ground shook under his feet. He wasn't sure if he was screaming. Even if he was, he knew no one would hear him. He couldn't even hear himself.

Then, as quickly as it had begun, the blasts ended. Alex opened his eyes and looked around at his friends, seeing their shocked faces mirroring his own fear. He could see Sol's lips moving but couldn't hear him. There was only the sound of ringing in his ears, as if he were up in a church tower and all the bells were being struck.

Locke appeared at the door and entered the studio. He, too, was speaking, but Alex could still hear nothing but the insistent ringing. Something touched his shoulder and he turned to see Abby, eyes wide, mouthing questions he couldn't understand. He felt an object being pressed into his right hand and his fingers closed automatically, unthinkingly around it. His eyes looked down to see what he was now holding.

It was a laz-pistol. He shook his head, trying to clear his brain as the ringing in his ears continued unabated. Locke was handing weapons to Abby and Tom and Harriet and Sol. They, too, seemed shocked, dumbstruck, at the assault on their senses. But Locke was all action. He tugged at Tom's arm, at the same time motioning for them to follow him. But Tom appeared as paralyzed as Alex.

Abby was the first to react, following Locke and leading the others as they staggered into the room with the mixing desk and the other gear. Alex felt shards of glass grinding under his boots. He noticed that the window separating the two rooms was gone, evidently shattered into a thousand pieces.

Locke shouted again. This time Alex could just make out the words, as if they were coming from someone yelling a long way away.

"We need to escape!" Again, Locke, motioned for them to follow.

Alex shook his head once more, still trying to clear his brain. A dim realization occurred to him: they were being attacked. Those sounds were bombs or missiles. He felt foolish for not figuring this out before. His brain still felt detached from his body, as if this was all happening to someone else.

Locke led them to the main door of the building. Tugging it open, he stuck his head out, but instantly pulled it back inside as a laser beam smashed into the doorframe just inches from his face. Without pausing, the old man kneeled down, pulled out a laz-pistol, put his hand outside, and returned fire, blazing away blindly in the direction from which the enemy blast had come. Two more beams of light struck close to Locke, missing him by mere inches, before the attack stopped. After waiting a few seconds, Locke risked another peek out the door.

Apparently satisfied they were no longer in imminent danger, he got to his feet, motioning once more for them to follow him outside.

But Locke was wrong. As the group rushed into the open, a military vehicle appeared from the trail ahead, driving rapidly towards them. It had a laz-cannon mounted on its roof. The weapon was pointing straight at them. And the man aiming it was General Slade Arnold.

45 | Battlefield Reunion

Alex braced himself for the inevitable, for Arnold to squeeze the trigger and blast them to pieces. Even from here, he could see the joy of battle, the jubilation of victory in Arnold's eyes as the vehicle began to brake, screeching to a halt less than thirty yards away, the weapon trained directly on them. Alex tried to move, to pull Abby away to safety all the time knowing it was too late, knowing they were sitting ducks for Arnold's deadly weapon.

A blast of fiery light lit up the clearing. For a moment, Alex thought it had come from the laz-cannon. Then he realized; it was aimed *at* the cannon.

The beam of light smashed into Arnold's weapon, hurling it off its mounting and sending it tumbling to the ground. Arnold was enveloped in a pall of smoke as a figure darted from out of the trees towards them.

It was Captain Bailey. She was shouting at them—screaming at them. This time, some of her speech cut through the ringing in his ears, like a malfunctioning microphone that only amplifies half the words.

"... your office. ... rear door. ... path ... river. ... only chance ..."

Locke obviously heard her instructions better than Alex, for he instantly began to lead them in the direction of the nearby building. As they rushed through the entrance, Alex cast one quick glimpse over his shoulder and saw Captain Bailey and two of her troopers sheltering behind a low wall, firing furiously at the vehicle and other unseen enemies.

Locke led them past the entrance hall and into the largest room—the one Alex had seen the team of techies working in only two days earlier. He started towards the corridor that led to Locke's office, then pulled up short as a figure emerged from out of the corridor, saw them, and aimed a laz-rifle at the group. Instantly, Locke and Sol lifted their weapons.

"Oh, it's you, sir," said the figure, addressing Locke. Alex recognized the uniform worn by Captain Bailey's troops. "You can't go this way, they're—"

Fzzoom!

A flash of light lit up the corridor as a laser bolt smashed into the young soldier's back, flinging him forward into the room. He landed face-first on the floor, lifeless and unmoving, by Alex's feet. A thin tendril of smoke snaked up from his blackened jacket.

"Get down!" Locke roared and this time Alex heard him clearly as the old man pushed Alex roughly aside and out of the line of fire. Alex stumbled and fell behind a desk, which shook as a laser blasted into it. Meanwhile, Locke and the others had taken shelter behind desks and chairs and were returning fire as beams of deadly light bounced off the walls and ceiling.

"Back to the entrance," Locke shouted as he started inching backwards the way they'd just come. The group had only just begun their retreat, however, when a scream issued from the corridor, then another, and the firing stopped.

"Don't shoot ... it's us!" bellowed a voice Alex recognized. Iggy appeared at the entrance to the corridor, weapon in hand. A millisec later and Iggy's mom had joined him, along with Leah Mecon and Abby's mom. Then, to his immense relief, Alex's mom emerged, followed a moment later by Ben.

"Good – you're here," Iggy said, scanning the group. "I took care of those guys," he said nodding back towards the corridor. "Now what?"

"The river," Locke replied. "Is that corridor clear?"

"Yes," Iggy replied. "But not for long. They're everywhere."

As if to prove his point, a barrage of laser blasts started up from out of the corridor as the group flung themselves once more behind desks and other office furniture. Iggy leaped to the side and slammed the door to the corridor shut, then locked it.

"That'll hold them for a while," Iggy declared.

"Yes, but it won't hold me." The voice came from the entrance hall on the other side of the room.

As Alex and the others whirled around, weapons ready, a man emerged from the shadows. He was flanked by half-a-dozen shadowy figures—six Fixers, all armed.

It was General Arnold again. And he had a look of triumph on his face.

46 | Iggy's Secret

"There's no need to fire," General Arnold said, looking calmly at the group and making a show of holstering his weapon. "Here, let me get my people to stop shooting at that door." He spoke quietly into a headset and the noise of lasers smashing and splintering the door into the corridor abruptly ended. "See? Nothing to fear," he declared, smiling magnanimously at the group, his hands open in a gesture of conciliation.

No one spoke as the two sides stared at each other. Outside, Alex could dimly make out the sound of weapons firing and people screaming. In the distance came the *whup-whup-whup* of a helicopter. A couple more Fixers appeared behind Locke, easing their way silently into the room, their faces in shadow, their weapons held in readiness.

"What happened to Captain Bailey?" Abby asked, breaking the silence.

"She is a casualty of war, Abigail Adams," General Arnold said, sounding almost regretful.

"How do you know my—"

"Your name? Oh, I have known all about you for some time, Ms. Adams. I'm surprised Locke hasn't—"

"What do you want, Arnold?" Locke cut in. "As you can see, we are at a stand-off."

"Not exactly, John. I have the building surrounded. The real question is, how would you like to leave here; in handcuffs or body bags?"

"He's lying. We can take them," Iggy said confidently, his gun at the ready as two more Fixers appeared behind General Arnold.

"That would be a mistake, Iggy Elgar. There is no way out. Why risk injury or even death when you can walk out with your head held high?"

"In chains?" Locke asked, sounding almost amused.

"For you, John, yes. But it does not have to be that way for Iggy."

There was silence.

"Why Iggy?" Abby asked, her voice shaking slightly.

"I will make you an offer, Abigail Adams," Arnold said, ignoring her question. "Since I am feeling magnanimous today, I will let all the young people leave here without handcuffs. Not just Iggy; all of you. All you need do is lay down your weapons. The adults, will, I'm afraid, need to be restrained. I'm sure you understand."

"But why Iggy? Why did you single him out first?" Abby persisted.

"Has your precious mentor not told you that, either?" Arnold said, his lips curling into a mocking smile as he looked from Abby to Locke and back again. "How curious. What other secrets is he keeping, I wonder?"

"I am not keeping secrets," Locke said, sounding exasperated. "I am simply trying to find the best time to share what little I know."

"You don't have to share anything with me, old man. I already know," Iggy said quietly. The others turned to stare at him.

"So you've figured it out, have you?" Arnold asked, smiling triumphantly. "Well done. Very well done! So, you know who you are?"

"Yes," Iggy replied, looking penetratingly at General Arnold, his face mask-like, his expression unreadable. "And I also know who you are … father."

47 | The End

"He's your dad?" Abby asked, gazing at Iggy in disbelief.

Iggy didn't answer. He just stared at the ground, his hand clutching the laz-pistol tightly.

"Iggy, did you hear me? Is that man really your father?"

"Yes," Iggy admitted at last, his voice flat and unemotional.

Iggy's mom let out a cry and put a hand to her mouth.

"Alice." General Arnold's voice sounded soft, his tone gentle, as he looked at her. "Do you remember me?"

Alice Elgar was gazing at Slade Arnold as if a veil had been lifted, her blue eyes wide, her breath coming in ragged gasps.

"Sly? Is that you?" she asked at last.

Slade Arnold nodded and held her gaze before finally tearing his eyes away.

"And now will the rest of you please put down your weapons? You will come to no harm, I promise," Arnold said, turning his gaze on the others.

"And you expect us to believe you?" Abby said fiercely.

"Why not? I have been more honest with you than your beloved Dr. Locke, haven't I? Do you even know who *he* really is?"

Alex turned to Locke. What was Arnold saying? Is this what Locke had been about to tell Alex the other day?

"I know who he is," Abby said quietly, casting a quick glance at John Locke. But the old man did not return her look; he was still staring angrily at Arnold.

"And just because you told us one secret doesn't mean I trust you," Abby continued, glaring angrily at the general. "You've lied and cheated before. You're evil. No way will I surrender to you."

"Neither will I," Tom said, stepping forward to stand beside Abby.

One-by-one, the others moved to form a single line with Abby. Finally, only Alice and Iggy remained off to one side.

"Even you, Liz?" Arnold said, looking at Alex's mom as she joined the others. "But then, you always were one to take the moral high ground."

"Do I … know you?" Liz asked, looking at Arnold and frowning, eyes narrowed.

"I could explain everything if you'd only surrender," General Arnold replied, still shaking his head slowly and looking from one member of the group to the next. "It is unfortunate you will not accept my offer, because I really—"

He never finished his sentence. Without warning, Abby raised her weapon and began to fire into the mass of Fixers. A millisec later, Tom, Sol, Alex, Harriet, and Leah had joined them, firing on the enemy while dropping into cover behind a large desk. Off to Alex's left, Locke, Susanna, Liz, and Ben ducked behind an old filing cabinet and began blasting away. The Fixers shot back as more joined the fight, advancing cautiously over fallen comrades. Lasers ricocheted off the walls.

It was mayhem. Ben fell as two beams blasted him simultaneously in the chest and head. Alex tried to crawl over to assist his mom as she leaned over him, but the beams of deadly light were too intense for Alex to cover the open space between them. Beside him, Abby was mouthing words Alex couldn't hear above the screams of weapons and humans.

Two Fixers burst out from the corridor behind them, the locked door now blasted into atoms by their fierce onslaught. Alex shot at one and hit him on the second attempt, while the other fell to Abby's gun. To his left, Locke was firing again and again, looking as calm as if he was on a firing range on a pleasant Sunday afternoon as Fixer after Fixer fell to his precise aim. To his right, Tom lifted his head and pointed his gun only to fall backwards, apparently hit. He lay there unmoving as Sol reached out to him, fear etched on his fine features. But there was nothing Alex and the others could do to help, for still the Fixers came, their weapons blazing, pinning them in place.

There were just too many, too many for Locke or Abby or any of them. Alex turned to Abby, who was firing blind, her hand round the side of the desk, trying to stay out of sight. She looked at him, despair in her eyes.

It was over. He knew it. She knew it.

Rage and a desperate hopelessness hit Alex in equal measure. They had come so close. Just a few minutes more and they would have broadcast their music. America would have been free, the malevolent MeChip overthrown.

But they had failed. Now people would live as chipslaves forever. How had Arnold found them, anyway? It didn't matter now, Alex realized.

Fury blossomed inside him. His head felt like it would explode. It would not finish like this. Not with him hiding behind a desk, skulking in fear as he waited for his inevitable end. No, he would fight the enemy face-to-face, standing up to them, head held high.

He took a deep breath and leaped to his feet, a wordless yell of defiance issuing from his lips as he fired furiously at his foes. Fixers were everywhere and Alex and his friends were outnumbered, but still his onslaught took them by surprise. His first shot hit one enemy in the chest, hurling him against a wall, where he crumpled to the ground. His second struck one in the thigh, while a third was hit in the side of his head, slamming him against a comrade, who dropped his weapon.

Lasers blasted back and one smashed into Alex's ankle, almost toppling him over. He staggered as pain seared up his leg, but still he fought on. Abby was now by his side, standing with him shoulder-to-shoulder. Then Locke, too, was on his feet, aiming and shooting, aiming and shooting.

But there were too many. It could not last. Their actions were hopeless ... doomed.

Alex never saw who fired the final shot. It smashed into his chest, lifting him into the air. For a millisec he felt weightless, as if he was flying free, soaring up into the atmosphere, perhaps to float away and escape this fiery hell forever. He hung for a moment, suspended, like a puppet on a string, before crashing back to earth, his body broken, his light gone out as the darkness claimed him.

48 | Home

Alex opened his eyes. He felt groggy and disoriented. He had just had the weirdest dream. There had been a forest and guns and a guitar and an old man and ... what else? As he tried to recall it more precisely the details seemed to seep out of his memory, like sand between his fingers. Finally, he gave up. It was only a dream. Reality was what mattered.

He sat up in bed, yawned, stretched, and pushed the covers aside. Pulling on his clothes, he glanced for a millisec at the posters of athletes and actors adorning his bedroom walls before heading downstairs for breakfast.

His mom wasn't there but his dad was just sitting down for his morning coffee.

"Good morning. Sleep well, son?"

"Okay, I guess."

Alex helped himself to cereal and a glass of milk. He checked the clock on the wall: 7:07. He must have forgotten to set his alarm. He'd better get a move on. He wolfed down his breakfast and raced back to his room, taking the stairs two at a time and almost crashing into his mom, who was emerging from the bathroom.

"Hey, what's the rush?"

"Training," he replied, not waiting for a response. He shoved his gear into his bag and bounded back down the stairs, yelled a quick farewell to his parents, and raced out the door. Fifteen minutes later he was at school. His friends Sol and Tom were waiting for him by the entrance.

"Nearly late again," Sol said, shaking his head.

"Nearly, but not quite," Alex replied, winking.

They made their way up the broad marble steps and through the sparkling steel-and-glass entrance into the hallway, heading towards the changing rooms. Five minutes later they were on the track with a dozen others warming up. Coach Elkins joined them.

"Listen up, everyone. The inter-school athletics meet is in three weeks and we all know what that means, right?"

"What does it mean, Coach?" Tom asked, frowning.

"It means more training, Mr. Hamilton, if you're to stand any chance of winning your event. Now, let's start with some stretches ..."

"Remind me why we quit music again?" Tom groaned as he emerged from the shower an hour later, rubbing his aching legs.

"We all agreed this was more fun," Sol said solemnly.

Tom looked like he was about to argue, then his expression brightened. "I guess so. Hey, did you see Martha and Sally watching us from the stands?"

"No," Sol said, shaking his head. "I was too busy training."

"I did. That Sally is pretty tidy, huh?"

They reached the classroom a few minutes later and had just taken their usual spots near the window, second row from the back, when their elderly English teacher, Ms. Monroe, entered the room, her left arm still in a cast from her recent accident.

"Good morning, everyone. Today we're going to begin a new project: the works of American novelist Mark Twain. Please pull up page one of *Tom Sawyer* on your MeChips."

Slade Arnold took a deep breath, smoothed his hair one last time, and entered the room. He stared at the figure seated behind the desk, waiting for her to look up. As soon as she did he gave her a smart salute.

"At ease, General. Charles, Edward, you may leave us," she said dismissing her two aides with a wave of her hand. "And close the door behind you."

Alone now with the woman behind the desk, Slade Arnold cast his eyes briefly around the room. The Oval Office was just as he remembered: the luxurious blue carpet, mustard-colored curtains, plush tan couches, flags, and small bookshelf on the right. Photographs of the president's late father and other family adorned the desk.

President Davora Davison stood up and walked towards him, installing herself on one of the couches. "Please sit," she instructed, smiling.

General Arnold moved to sit on the other couch but the president held up a hand.

"Not there ... here," she said, motioning next to her.

Arnold sat down, turning to look at her once more. He had to admit: even up close she was as beautiful as ever.

"So, Slade, what news?" she asked, still smiling.

"All of them have been caught, Madam President."

"Madam President? Since when did you call me that, Slade? Come now, you must always call me Davora. But continue, please."

"Everyone was caught in the operation ... Davora."

"Good. And have you disposed of them in the usual manner?"

"No."

"Oh. You're trying the medical option again, are you? The brain surgery?"

"Not this time."

"Then what?" she asked, her smile fading slightly.

"I've installed new MeChips and reprogrammed them. They're back in their old lives. With a few modifications, of course."

"You reprogrammed them? Nothing more? You think that will work after such a traumatic experience?"

"I'm sure it will, Davora. The control we can achieve with the new MeChip coding and AI enhancements, the improvements we've—"

"Really? This is not your usual style, Slade. You don't think it's a risk?"

"Not at all. We're monitoring them carefully to see if the rehabilitation works. We can always intervene if needed."

"And the musical threat?"

"Taken care of. None of those involved in the plot have any interest in music now."

"I see." President Davison was silent for several seconds, her lips pursed in contemplation. Finally, she spoke again.

"Are you sure you're not too close to all of this, Slade?"

"No, Davora. This is all purely professional. And I assure you, it will work. They were mostly kids, anyway; victims of Locke's brainwashing. It hasn't been hard to fix their memories," he said, trying to sound casual and in control as a bead of sweat formed on his forehead.

"Well, Slade, I'll leave it in your very capable hands. But make sure you keep a close eye on things. We don't want any further mistakes or, worse, people thinking you're going soft ... losing your touch."

"Of course. Trust me," he said, swallowing.

"Oh, Slade, naturally I trust you. After everything we've been through together, how could I not?" She laughed, her voice playful and light. "I know you won't let me down," she added, placing a hand on his arm.

Slade Arnold looked into her face. Her voice still sounded good-humored and lively, her smile remained broad and kind. But her eyes—those piercing eyes that had beguiled and bewitched an entire nation—were as cold and hard as death.

49 | Love and Hate

Alex was exhausted. The last month had been busier than any he could remember. His teachers seemed to have decided December was not a time for gifts and goodwill but tests and hard work, as they all piled on extra homework and surprise quizzes in class.

Meanwhile, athletics training was getting more intense. To his immense surprise and delight, Alex had won the 3000 meters inter-school race and placed second in the 5k. His friends had done well, too: Tom had secured a silver medal in the 10k, while Sol had garnered the bronze in both the discus and the 200 meters.

Coach Elkins had rewarded them with even more training sessions before and after school. "Now you're all winners, you need to stay winners," he'd said after announcing the new regime.

While Alex may have gone to bed exhausted, it didn't seem to improve his sleep. Every night he had the same dream: there was a forest in it, a lurking, imminent danger, and a lot of noise. While he slept it felt to him like it was all very important. Yet when he woke the memory of it always slipped away from him too fast for it to make any sense at all.

He also awoke every morning with a strong desire to train, to run. His athletics was becoming more important to him as each week passed, a passion bordering on obsession. Fortunately, Sol and Tom seemed to feel the same way. None of them minded the extra training. "We're athletes now," Tom declared as they got dressed after another session. "Which makes us pretty cool."

"Tom, you'll always be a dexter," Sol replied.

"No way! That girl Sally definitely likes me. Why would she be interested in me if I was a dexter, huh? And did you notice how Martha keeps checking you out, Alex?"

"Not really," Alex replied. Still, he thought, Tom could be right. Sally *was* around a lot when they were training. Not only that, but her friend Martha had joined her several times and always made a point of saying hi to Alex.

"Speaking of girls, did you hear Charlotte Riedesel is going out with Iggy Elgar?" Tom said.

"I thought they'd broken up way back?" Sol replied.

"Apparently they're together again. Personally, I don't get why the star quarterback and school chess champion would date, but I guess when Cupid strikes love is blind," Tom said, waxing lyrical.

"In your case, it'd have to be," Sol said.

"Hey ... not funny!" Tom protested, whipping at Sol's legs with his towel.

Two days before the end-of-year holidays were due to start, Alex was walking down the corridor to the cafeteria for lunch. For once he was by himself, having been delayed by their English teacher Ms. Monroe, who'd wanted to speak with him about his essay on *Tom Sawyer*. He hoped Sol and Tom had saved him a seat.

He was passing one of the music rooms when on an impulse he paused, opened the door, and walked inside. It was already half empty, as the music department was soon to close permanently. Still, a few rows of instruments remained, packed carefully on shelves around the walls. He spotted a couple of guitars and a memory of his previous playing returned, unbidden. He'd decided to quit music only a month earlier but suddenly felt an odd longing, an almost irresistible urge, to play once more.

He strolled slowly forward, picked up a guitar, and connected it to a small amp. He ran his fingers and thumb across the strings, picking out chords. A wave of emotion caught him as he caressed the instrument and started to play. He'd almost forgotten how good it was to make music, forgotten how much joy he could—

"Aaaaaargh!"

Alex screamed in pain. His head felt like it would explode, his fingers were on fire. The sudden assault on his senses was so excruciating he almost passed out. Reeling, he dropped the guitar and stumbled from the room, his palms pressed against his temples as he sought to escape, to get away from that place of torture, to flee that guitar. He staggered down the corridor and into the nearest boys' bathroom where he dragged himself into a cubicle and retched once, then a second time.

As quickly as it had arrived, the pain promptly passed, leaving him shaken and scared. What had he been thinking, playing music again? How could he have forgotten that he hated playing music now … hated it so much! He never wanted to play an instrument again, ever. Athletics was his thing these days. It always would be. And he was good at it, too. He loved it. Just loved it. As he thought about running a wave of calm, of tranquility, washed over him.

He took a few deep breaths, unlocked the cubicle door, and washed his face and hands. Feeling almost back to his old self, he headed out into the corridor, checking his MeChip as he did so to make sure he still had enough time to join the others for lunch.

50 | Awake

Three weeks later and the memory of that awful experience with the guitar had faded. Instead, all of Alex's focus these days was on his running. He was feeling exhilarated as he got home that Tuesday evening. He'd just run a personal best in training and was tired but happy. He'd sleep well that night for sure.

"Sorry I'm late—Coach Elkins kept us longer than usual," he announced as he walked into the kitchen.

"That's fine, Alex. Perfect timing, actually. Dinner's just ready," said his dad, who was dishing out food onto three plates.

"Hi, Alex. How was your day?" his mom asked as she entered the room a millisec later.

"Good. I just ran a PB in the 3000 meters."

"That's great!" both parents declared at once. After a few minutes of chat, the three of them lapsed into a companionable silence; his mom pulled a book out of her bag, Alex checked his MeChip for messages, and his father resumed reading the old-fashioned newspaper he still insisted on having delivered each day.

"Hon, did you see this?" asked his dad, pointing to an article in the paper.

"What's that, darling?" Alex's mom replied, looking up for a millisec from her book.

"That guy Locke who started the fire last month. He's escaped."

"Really?" his mom asked, although she only sounded half-interested as her eyes strayed back to her novel.

"Yeah. On the run. Here's his picture. He looks too old to have broken out of a high-security prison, don't you think?" he said, holding up the black-and-white image for Alex and his mom to see.

Alex glanced up, more from politeness than anything else, and stared in shock. His heart began beating rapidly.

"Are you alright, Alex?"

"I'm not sure—"

"You don't have to worry about this guy. It's not like he's here in the room," his dad said, laughing. "And anyway, he's ancient. He couldn't harm us even if he did ever return to Lincoln."

"No, of course. You're right. I'm fine," Alex said, trying to compose his features back into a semblance of normalcy "Hey listen, I'm done with my dinner so am just gonna go upstairs and do my homework, okay?"

"Of course, Alex," both parents said at once.

Alex stood up, took his plate and cutlery to the sink, rinsed them, and put them in the dishwasher. As he left the room, he sneaked one last peak at the man in the newspaper before heading upstairs to his bedroom. He sat on his bed, closed his eyes, and concentrated. Hard. His mind felt like it was on the edge of something ... something important. It felt tantalizingly close but out of reach, like a name you know you know but can't quite remember. He wracked his brain for at least ten minutes, desperately trying to recall where he'd seen that face before.

It wouldn't come. Finally, he gave up and turned to his still-incomplete homework.

He awoke with a start. It was almost pitch black, with not a sign of the sun's light, not even a hint dawn might be close. Yet Alex felt wide awake. Without thinking what he was doing he climbed out of bed and tiptoed quietly onto the upstairs landing. He made his way carefully down the steps—avoiding the one that creaked near the bottom—and entered the kitchen, closing the door carefully behind him before he turned on the light.

There on the table lay the newspaper. He approached it almost fearfully, picked it up, and started riffling through the pages until he came upon the photo.

He gazed at it for a long time, unable to tear his eyes away, seemingly frozen to the spot like one of Medusa's prey. The answer was in that elderly face, in the old man's eyes. He just knew it.

And then it hit him. With a jolt like an electric shock, the curtain on reality was ripped away and Alex remembered ... *everything*. Memories flooded back one after the other and he knew who this man was, knew *how* he knew him, knew it all; the forest, the music, his friends, Abby, Iggy, Locke, the Fixers, General Arnold. All of it assaulted his brain in one mad rush, threatening to overwhelm him like a tidal wave. Desperately he clung on, trying to retain his sense of sanity as thousands of images and memories washed over him, threatening to drown him. Gradually, however, they began to make sense, to form a picture he knew, a picture he understood.

His heart was racing and he felt exhausted, as if he'd just run another 5k race. He took a deep breath and sat down, still looking at the photograph intently.

Dr. John Locke. Where was he now, Alex wondered? And how had he, Alex, regained his true memories? His MeChip was still in, wasn't it? Carefully, he touched the back of his neck. Yes, it was still there, its rose-tinted world and insidious lies still busily gnawing away at his consciousness.

But he knew what it was now. He had remembered himself, remembered who he really was and what he had been trying to do.

He sat at that table for the next two hours, his mind whirling, his thoughts spinning. He thought about his parents, his friends, and

Abby; about Leah and Electa and all the people they'd met in Hope; about Maggie Corbin, the woman they'd encountered in the forest, and Francesca Delano, the president who never was; about Iggy and the secrets they'd begun to uncover; about Locke's plans to beat the MeChip and how it had all ultimately ended in their defeat by General Arnold. He thought of everything they had been through, about their dreams of freeing the country from the tyranny of that technology. He thought about the MeChip's incredible power … and its vulnerabilities.

Finally, as the first hints of morning began to tinge the sky, he made up his mind. Everything was clear. As clear as daylight.

The path forward would be perilous, he realized that. But it was obvious to him what needed to happen.

He had decided. And he knew just what he had to do next.

END OF BOOK 2

FROM THE AUTHOR

Dear reader,

Thank you for entering the world of *Rock Happy*. If you enjoyed *Rock Happy 2: Dissonant*, please consider reading **Rock Happy 3: Discordant,** in which Alex takes the fight to his enemies for a final showdown.

If you liked *Rock Happy 2,* I'd be so grateful if you'd take a moment to **leave a review** or rating from the online retailer where you got it. That way, you'll help others know about the series.

As our hero Alex might say—thanks so smeckin' much!

Chris Spence

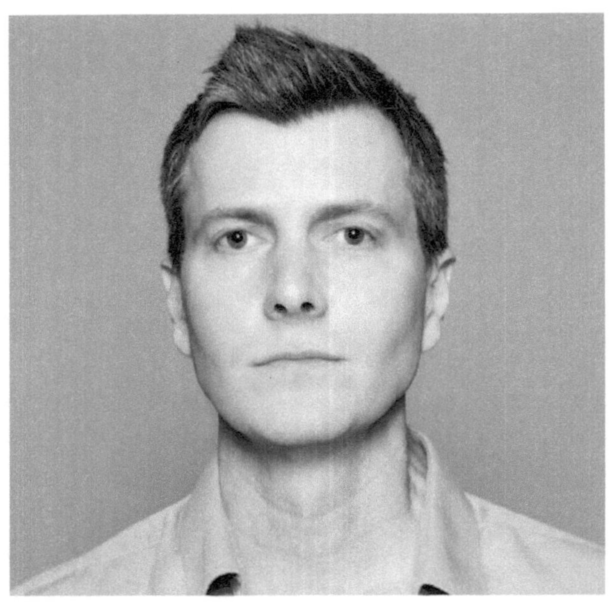

About the Author

From politics to rock bands, journalism to environmental advocacy, Chris draws on his past experiences to write intriguing fantasy and science fiction.An award-winning writer, Chris is currently working on his **Rock Happy** dystopian books and the **Skyrack Chronicles**, a fantasy series where the characters' favorite role playing game comes to life.Originally from England, Chris has since lived in New Zealand, New York, San Francisco, and Dublin, Ireland.

Read more at chrisspenceauthor.com.